TO THE SUN

BY TENNESSEE WILLIAMS

PLAYS

Baby Doll & Tiger Tail
Camino Real
Candles to the Sun
Cat on a Hot Tin Roof
Clothes for a Summer Hotel
Fugitive Kind
The Glass Menagerie
A Lovely Sunday for Creve Coeur
Not About Nightingales
The Notebook of Trigorin
Something Cloudy, Something Clear
Spring Storm
Stairs to the Roof
Stopped Rocking and Other Screen Plays
A Streetcar Named Desire
Sweet Bird of Youth

THE THEATRE OF TENNESSEE WILLIAMS, VOLUME I
Battle of Angels, A Streetcar Named Desire, The Glass Menagerie
THE THEATRE OF TENNESSEE WILLIAMS, VOLUME II
The Eccentricities of a Nightingale, Summer and Smoke, The Rose Tattoo, Camino Real
THE THEATRE OF TENNESSEE WILLIAMS, VOLUME III
Cat on a Hot Tin Roof, Orpheus Descending, Suddenly Last Summer
THE THEATRE OF TENNESSEE WILLIAMS, VOLUME IV
Sweet Bird of Youth, Period of Adjustment, The Night of the Iguana
THE THEATRE OF TENNESSEE WILLIAMS, VOLUME V
The Milk Train Doesn't Stop Here Anymore, Kingdom of Earth (The Seven Descents of Myrtle), Small Craft Warnings, The Two-Character Play
THE THEATRE OF TENNESSEE WILLIAMS, VOLUME VI
27 Wagons Full of Cotton and Other Short Plays
THE THEATRE OF TENNESSEE WILLIAMS, VOLUME VII
In the Bar of a Tokyo Hotel and Other Plays
THE THEATRE OF TENNESSEE WILLIAMS, VOLUME VIII
Vieux Carré, A Lovely Sunday for Creve Coeur, Clothes for a Summer Hotel, The Red Devil Battery Sign

27 Wagons Full of Cotton and Other Plays
The Two-Character Play
Vieux Carré

POETRY

Collected Poems
In the Winter of Cities

PROSE

Collected Stories
Hard Candy and Other Stories
One Arm and Other Stories
The Roman Spring of Mrs. Stone
The Selected Letters of Tennessee Williams, Volume I
The Selected Letters of Tennessee Williams, Volume II
Where I Live: Selected Essays

TENNESSEE WILLIAMS

CANDLES TO THE SUN

A PLAY IN TEN SCENES

EDITED, WITH AN INTRODUCTION,
BY DAN ISAAC

FOREWORD
BY WILLIAM JAY SMITH

A NEW DIRECTIONS BOOK

Candles to the Sun is published by special arrangement with The University of the South, Sewanee, Tennessee.

Book design by Sylvia Frezzolini Severance
Manufactured in the United States of America
New Directions Books are printed on acid-free paper.
First published as New Directions Paperbook 986 in 2004
Published simultaneously in Canada by Penguin Canada Books, Ltd.

Library of Congress Cataloging-in-Publication Data:

Williams, Tennessee, 1911-1983.
Candles to the sun : a play in ten scenes / by Tennessee Williams.
p. cm.
Includes bibliographical references.
ISBN 0-8112-1574-1 (acid-free paper)
1. Strikes and lockouts—Drama. 2. Poor families—Drama. 3. Labor unions—Drama. 4. Coal miners—Drama. 5. Alabama—Drama. I. Title.
PS3545.I5365C36 2004
812'.54—dc22

2003028151

New Directions Books are published for James Laughlin
by New Directions Publishing Corporation
80 Eighth Avenue, New York, NY 10011

CONTENTS

FOREWORD

BY WILLIAM JAY SMITH

I had the rare privilege of attending in St. Louis, on Saturday March 20, 1937, a performance of *Candles to the Sun*, the first full-length play of Tennessee Williams. The performance took place in the auditorium of the Wednesday Club, an elite women's cultural organization. The play had been produced by an amateur theatrical troupe, the Mummers, and directed by Willard Holland, who played one of the leading roles and, more importantly, had almost single-handedly helped to shape the final version of the play from the more than 400 unnumbered typewritten pages of various drafts that now repose at the Harry Ransom Humanities Research Center in Austin, Texas. This was the second of two performances, but the major one, of *Candles to the Sun*, which had had, we learn from the typescript, several other tentative titles, including *The Lamp*, *Place in the Sun*, and *Candles* in *the Sun*.

The primary focus of the Mummers was drama of social concern and this play, presenting as it does the travails and struggles of three generations of a family of coalminers in the Red Hills of Alabama, seemed definitely to fit the bill. The play appears now in these pages for the first time anywhere thanks to the fortuitous, wise, and thoughtful intervention of Jane Garrett, who played the important role of Star, the wayward daughter of this strict Puritanical coal-mining family, and Dan Isaac, who has meticulously edited and reconstructed the Mummers script. I trust that it will delight a worldwide audience of readers, and eventually theatergoers, as it did the perceptive newspaper critics and others in those small, but extremely enthusiastic, gatherings sixty-seven years ago. It was for me, not only a decided pleasure, but also an absolute revelation, all the more astonishing because I had come fully prepared, I thought, to give my heart-felt approval to any offering of my dear friend and close associate, Thomas Lanier Williams, however modest and unpolished it proved to be.

Dakin Williams, Tom's younger brother, together with his parents, had attended the Thursday, March 18th premiere (or preview, as the Mummers preferred to call it). He remembers that Tom had sat at some distance from his family and from most of the others in the audience, alone in an aisle seat, which he had insisted on having. When to thunderous applause, loud cheers, and resonant foot-stomping the full cast gathered for numerous curtain calls, they suddenly all burst out singing "Solidarity Forever." The celebrated union anthem, totally uncalled for in the script, gave the play an aura of propaganda, which the playwright, despite his pronounced sympathy for victims of social injustice, had clearly not intended.

I met Tom Williams at Washington University in St. Louis in 1935. He had come there after his father, Cornelius Coffin Williams (C.C.), a veteran of the Spanish-American War, horrified that Tom had flunked R.O.T.C. after three years at the University of Missouri, brought him back to St. Louis to work in the shoe factory where he was a sales manager. Tom had heart palpitations (he later referred to them as a heart attack), and since it was clear that he could not continue in this tedious, difficult job, he was permitted to register at Washington University as a Special Student. We were introduced by Clark Mills McBurney, who, as Clark Mills, had published widely in prominent magazines and who was studying for a Master's degree in French at the University. I had just registered there and as a freshman was immediately placed in advanced courses in French since early training had made me fairly proficient in that language. I made Clark's acquaintance at the first meeting of the College Poetry Society. Ann Winslow (her real name was Grubbs) had written to colleges and universities all over the country and had persuaded them to establish chapters. She raised money for prizes which were awarded by juries of prominent writers to young promising poets throughout the country. Clark introduced me to Tom, and after the three of us attended the next meeting of the College Poetry Society, we decided that we were the only ones in that organization truly interested in writing poetry, and from then on we met on our own, usually at Tom's house on Pershing Avenue, which was a ten-minute walk from the campus. I was the kid, the youngest of the group. Tom was seven years older than I and Clark, five. Because he seemed to have read everything that mattered in both French and English, Clark became our mentor. In my memoir *Army Brat* I have described Tom as he was at the time, one of the shyest men I'd ever known, very, very quiet and soft-spoken. Once he got to know someone he would let himself go, but otherwise he was quite withdrawn. His stony-faced silence often put people off, he appeared uninterested in what was going on around him, never joining in the quiet give-and-take of a conversation but rather listening carefully and taking it all in. He would sit quietly in a gathering for long periods of time until suddenly like a volcano erupting he would burst out with a high cackle and then with resounding and uncontrollable laughter. Tom's mother, who always graciously greeted us, was a busy little woman who never stopped talking although there wasn't much inflection or warmth in the steady flow of her speech. One topic, no matter how trivial, received the same emphasis as the next which might be utterly tragic. I had the impression listening to her that the words she pronounced were like the red balls in a game of Chinese checkers, all suddenly released and clicking quickly and aimlessly about the board.

Tom, Clark, and I were inseparable, meeting several times a week and spending evenings out with a number of attractive coeds (Clark had far more success with them than Tom or I). Although we confided constantly in one another, Tom kept any hint of depression to himself and with us appeared always tough-skinned, energetic, and above all determined to make a success as a writer and to get away as soon as possible from St. Louis, which was for him and for us an intolerable cultural backwater.

I knew, of course, that Tom had written plays, any number of short ones, each of which he usually referred to as a "fantasy." But for me at the time he was first and foremost a poet, and it was as a poet that I expected him to make a national name for himself. And indeed he did just that, but not for his poems as such but rather for the poetry of his plays, which was powerfully revealed to me in *Candles to the Sun.*

One of the most significant short "fantasy" plays of Tom's with which I became acquainted was *Me, Vashya.* In early 1937 Tom eagerly awaited the announcement of the three one-act play winners in the annual contest in English 16, Professor William G.B. Carson's "Technique of Modern Drama." English 16, the only writing course then offered at Washington University except for Professor Webster's in the short story, was quite popular on the campus. The students wrote one-act plays and at the end of the year three plays were chosen and given workshop productions. One of the three was selected as the best and its author was awarded fifty dollars, a considerable sum in those days, especially for students. Tom had received a B in the course for the first semester and after his play *Death of Pierrot* had failed to get even an honorable mention in the contest of the Webster Groves Theatre Guild the previous year, he was hoping he would fare better with Professor Carson. "Horrible if I were eliminated," he wrote in his journal. And horrible indeed it was when that elimination of his play *Me, Vashya* was announced.

I remember his bitterness at the time. The decision was said to have been that of an "independent jury" but Tom thought, as others of us did, that it was solely Professor Carson's, especially when the winner chosen for a full production was a play by Wayne Arnold, who appeared to be Carson's favorite in the class. His play *First Edition* was a drawing-room comedy concerning a recent winner of the Pulitzer Prize. Although not mentioned by name, this was the local author Josephine W. Johnson, whose lyrical novel *Now in November* Tom, Clark, and I very much admired. *First Edition*, a bright little piece, was the absolute opposite of Tom's somber dramatization of the murder of a powerful munitions maker who sold armaments to both sides in wartime. And war was much on everyone's mind. The assassination the previous summer of the poet-playwright Federico García Lorca by General Franco's Fascists in Spain enraged us all. Tom was attempting to deal with a large and very dark subject, and ironically it was precisely this subject, Professor Carson later revealed, that caused him to eliminate Tom's play. *Me, Vashya* may now seem, as apparently it did when read aloud in Carson's class, laughably melodramatic, but as the youthful fantastic treatment of a very real problem it was to us, his fellow beginning writers, serious and moving.

What was particularly hurtful to Tom about this defeat was that, while on the surface his subject appeared remote, he had put so much of himself and his own life into this play. Lady Shontine's madness is clearly a reflection of his sister Rose's mental breakdown which so haunted Tom at the time and the blunt, obsessive vulgarity of Vashya himself surely owed much to that of Tom's alcoholic father, who was making his sister's life and his own totally unbearable.

Tom Williams' next failure was a private rather than a public one. At about the time of Carson's rejection, Tom read to Clark and me the just-completed draft of what was apparently his first attempt at poetic drama. It was *Ishtar: A Babylonian Fantasy*. He had first tackled such an exotic subject in 1928 when at the age of seventeen, he wrote a short story, "The Vengeance of Nitocris," based on a paragraph of Herodotus. It tells of an Egyptian queen who avenges her father's murder by locking his murderers in an underground chamber while festivities take place overhead. It contains the memorable opening line: "Hushed were the streets of many-peopled Thebes." One would have thought that now at the age of twenty-six Tom would have left behind such attempts at Flaubertian exoticism, but no. Here presented to us in his rich Southern voice was a bit of Babylonian Gothic. This may have been the resurrection of a much earlier piece or a blind stab at verse drama that was then so popular. In any case, he did not get very far with his reading before Clark and I exploded with laughter. Tom responded not by clamming up, mute and hurt, but rather immediately joining in with his celebrated cackle, astonished himself that he could have seriously set down such patent nonsense.

I found only one page remaining of *Ishtar* in the Harry Ransom Humanities Research Center in Austin, Texas. I quote from it only to show how very far Tom had come with the truly spare and moving poetry in every line of *Candles to the Sun*.

Ishtar
(*A Babylonian Fantasy*)

Ishtar that naked walked
Beyond the seventh gate of Hell for Tammuz sake
Has heard my prayer!
Let us be wanton then! Give me your lips!
Give me your saffron-scented lips. . .
What's this!
Oh, here's a sorry end! My lover sleeps.

And then a few lines farther on:

I see the silver arrow of the dawn on the heels of the night.

Hail, Dawn! I salute you!
Hail, rising sun!
Hail Ever-Conquering Worm That Eats All But the Sky!

For a less florid effort, "Sonnets for the Spring," Tom received first prize in a poetry contest at the Wednesday Club. The award was presented to him on his birthday, March 26, 1936, in the same auditorium where *Candles to the Sun* would appear almost exactly a year later. It had been established in 1925 by the celebrated lyric poet Sara Teasdale, whom Tom greatly admired. He was aware that in 1914 after rejecting the proposal of poet Vachel Lindsay, she had married Ernst Filsinger, a highly successful international St. Louis businessman who made and sold shoes. She divorced him in 1929, and four years later, having found life in St. Louis intolerable, took an overdose of sleeping pills and was found dead in her bathtub. Tom had been very moved by her suicide and had written an ode to her, "Under April Rain."

He turned again to April, that cruelest of months, in his prize-winning sonnets. The first of these, "Singer of Darkness," serves as a fitting prelude to *Candles to the Sun* because it deals, as does the play, with the struggle between light and dark:

Singer of Darkness

I feel the onward rush of spring once more
Breaking upon the unresistant land
And foaming up the dark hibernal shore
As turbulent waves unfurled on turbid sand!
The cataclysm of the uncurled leaf,
The soundless thunder of the bursting green
Stuns every field. The sudden war is brief,
And instantly the flag of truce is seen,
The still, white blossom raised upon the bough!
(Singer of darkness, oh, be silent now!
Raise no defense, dare to erect no wall,
But let the living fire, the bright storm fall
With lyric paeans of victory once more
Against your own blindly surrendered shore!)

Reed Hynds, reviewing *Candles to the Sun* for the *St. Louis Star-Times,* contended it was certainly not a propaganda play, as some "lobby critics" had thought, but rather "an earnest and searching examination of a particular social reality set out in human and dramatic terms." In a separate interview in the same paper, Tom had explained that "the candles [in the title of the] play represent the individual lives of the people. The sun represents group consciousness. The play ends as a tragedy for the individuals, for in the end they realize they cannot achieve success and happiness apart from the group but must sacrifice for the common good." I think at the same time that for Tom this had not only a social but also a personal reference. John Donne, a poet whom Tom particularly appreciated, had written, "No man is an island, entire of itself; every man is a piece of the continent, a part of the main," and these lines might well be an epigraph for *Candles to the Sun*. Tom, speaking personally, referred at the time to the "Island of Myself," and it was, he later declared, to ward off the dread of loneliness that he wrote. If he was an island, he knew that, in his life as in his work, he had to create a bridge to humanity, to a greater world beyond the self.

If taken only literally as a chronicle of social protest, the play can never be fully understood. It must be read as a closely unified and carefully developed metaphor. It is an extended study of light and dark, both inside and outside the characters and the setting. The action moves, as does the sonnet, "Singer of Darkness," from dark into light, with all the degrees of chiaroscuro and shadow along the way. The two principal pivotal characters are the heroines, Star, the miner Bram Pilcher's daughter, and Fern, his daughter-in-law. Note the careful choice of names, each with its own metaphorical implication. Star moves from her virginal purity that like the real star above her cuts clearly through the camp's darkness, drawn by her own sensuality to the false bright light of Birmingham, the urban dark. She loses her chance to regain that innocence when Red, the spiritual organizer she loves, is murdered. She turns then to the brothel that had always awaited her and from which she will send some of the dark money she earns to help Fern, ironically, purchase freedom from the mine and light for young Luke, her son, whose name means light. Fern, on the other hand, like the plant for which she is named, grows up out of darkness into light: her clean pure self is aware that she can move from her grief and her dark inner self into the blinding, liberating light of the sun. To obtain the greater freedom that the strike provides for the entire community, Fern sacrifices all that she has strived for. The final scene with Fern transcendent in the rocking chair and light streaming through the open door is heartbreaking in its intensity. This intensity is prepared for us by the stage directions of the final scene that are in themselves pure poetry: *Winter has broken up and it is now one of those clear, tenuous mornings in early spring. A thin, clear sunlight pale as lemon-water comes through the windowpanes of the cabin which is now barer and cleaner-looking than usual in this strange light.* Heartbreaking also at the same time is Bram, the "Old Man of the Mines" who has preferred to remain in the dark, to go down daily into the dirt to dig his own grave, a mole who knows nothing but the dark and is blinded by sunlight. He moves finally into a deeper level of the dark, into the madness from which there is no return.

It is what Henry James calls "the madness of art" that saves Tom from the madness that he contemplated in his sister, and that he so feared would overtake him as well. The ghost of Rose hovers over this entire play, rising as from the heavy morning mist that Luke sees, "thick as wood smoke down on the hollow." Fern and Star are both aspects of Tom's imaginative vision of Rose: Fern, evoking her enduring and transcendent innocence; Star, an innocence lost to a destructive sensuality of the powerful sort that he felt had brought on Rose's madness.

Clark has told that he and I attended the Saturday performance of *Candles to the Sun* with the "underground crew" of our rebellious Bohemian confrères. Among them may have been the star members of the League of Artists and Writers whom Tom had met when he attended their weekly meetings in 1936 at the old courthouse near the St. Louis riverfront: poet Orrick Johns, novelist (and Marxist) Jack Conroy, short-story writer J.S. Balch, and humorist Willie Wharton. Whether or not they were all there I am not sure, but I have the distinct recollection that we all went on, along with Tom, to the apartment of Jack Conroy where we spent the rest of the night with some tough heavy-drinking types I had never before encountered. Clark had this memory of Tom that night:

> He was there at the beginning of the show, but at the intermission Tom was gone—nobody could find him. Finally, I found him outside. It was a cold night—he was sitting on the curbstone in front of the theatre with a bottle of whiskey—and he was drunk as a skunk and in total despair. Apparently, something had gone wrong, or he imagined it. I know he was intensely concerned with the reaction of audiences, and now suddenly he saw the play as hopeless, and he was drinking himself into oblivion. He refused to go back in—he saw it as just a total disaster. That was the only time I ever saw him really drunk.

I have a feeling, now that I have examined the play carefully and know much more about its author than I did then, that it may not have been that something had gone wrong in the production but that it was simply too painful for him to watch a play in which he had put so much of himself and his sister. Of *The Glass Menagerie* he said late in his life: "It is the saddest play I have ever written. It is full of pain. It is painful for me to see it." To my mind *Candles to the Sun* is also one of Tom's saddest plays, full of pain, but one of the most beautiful. It now deserves a place beside *The Glass Menagerie*.

May 2004

INTRODUCTION

BY DAN ISAAC

By early 1936, Thomas Lanier Williams III (1911-1983) had become well known in a small circle of young St. Louis bohemian literati as an accomplished poet whose work was starting to gain wider attention. On March 26th, his twentieth-fifth birthday, his "Sonnets for the Spring" won a prestigious competition created by the late St. Louis poet Sara Teasdale. As though the fates had conspired to confirm Tom Williams in his calling as a poet, a letter arrived at just the same time from Harriet Monroe, famed editor of *Poetry* magazine, informing him that she would publish two of his poems during the coming year. In a letter dated March 27, 1936, Williams graciously declared that he was "surprised and delighted."

At that moment it seemed clear the young Tom Williams was destined to realize his dream of becoming a self-impoverished poet. But 1936 turned out to be the year Williams decided to write for the theater—though he continued to write poetry all his life. The result of this shift was a full-length play, *Candles to the Sun*, produced in 1937 by the Mummers of St. Louis (under the direction of Willard Holland) and published here for the first time. But how to account for his new interest in playwriting?

Tom Williams had entered the University of Missouri in 1929 to attend the famed School of Journalism. In the spring of 1930, Professor Robert Ramsay sensed something special about the freshman who was auditing his course in modern drama, and urged him to write a play and enter it in the university-sponsored annual one-act play contest. Williams heeded this advice and wrote *Beauty Is the Word*. Despite the play's rhetoric and didacticism, it was credited for its original plot (concerning a puritanical missionary on a South Sea Island and his visiting niece whose "God is beauty"), with the judges awarding it sixth place and honorable mention. The following year, 1931, Williams entered *Hot Milk at Three in the Morning*, a play about a man filled with wanderlust who feels trapped by his wife and their newborn baby. The play took 13th place and was not awarded honorable mention. Neither play received a production, which was one of the possible rewards of the contest. However, later on, *Moony's Kid Don't Cry*, a rewritten and renamed version of *Hot Milk,* was submitted by Williams with four or five other one-act plays under the rubric title of *American Blues* to a Group Theatre play contest in 1938, and not only won a special monetary award, but gained the attention of Audrey Wood, who became his agent.

* * *

In June 1932, Tom Williams' often harsh father, Cornelius Coffin Williams, dealt his son's hopes and plans a devastating blow. Tom Williams had wanted to become a journalist upon graduation, which would have permitted him to escape a home that his mother and father had turned into a hateful marital battleground. Even more important, as a working journalist he would have had the opportunity to sharpen his reporting skills, with time left over for his true love: writing poetry and short stories. But when C.C., as his father was known, raised in military schools and a proud veteran of the 1898 Spanish-American War, received his son's report card and discovered that Tom had failed R.O.T.C., he informed his son that he would not permit him to return to the University of Missouri for his senior year.

Edwina Dakin Williams later provided a first-hand account of the event that prematurely terminated the first part of Williams' fractured college education:

> Tom's failing R.O.T.C. was like a slap in the face to his father. "I told you he's not doing any good in college," Cornelius stormed at me. "I'm going to take him out and

> put him to work." This was the third year of the Depression and Cornelius constantly felt the financial bottom dropping out of his world....He insisted Tom not return to the university for his final year. Tom wanted with all his heart to get a degree, to keep learning, to be able to write more effectively. . . . But he did not defy his father. I can only guess what this must have cost him psychically.[1]

Cornelius worked at the International Shoe Company where he got his son a job that paid $65 a month. Tom entered a world of dusting shoes, typing out factory orders, hauling packing cases stuffed with samples—the world of his father.

There is a melancholy postscript to Williams' aborted undergraduate career at the University of Missouri, and it came in the form of a deeply-felt letter from the Chairman of the English Department, Robert L. Ramsay, the same professor who had encouraged Tom to write his first play and enter it into a local competition. Dated December 10, 1932, the letter reads in part: "Your absence from the University this year has been a matter for real regret to all of us who knew the excellent work you did here the last few years, especially in the field of creative writing. I hope you will be able to return here and finish your course."

Williams worked at the International Shoe Company for nearly three years. After episodes of heart palpitations in early 1935—Williams always referred to them as heart attacks—he was finally able to quit the factory. The Williams family, rarely unified, met together to make the right decision for Tom's immediate future: he would spend the coming summer in Memphis with his dearly loved maternal grandparents, Episcopalian minister Reverend Walter Edwin Dakin and his wife Rose Otto Dakin, who had retired to Memphis in 1931, after serving at the church of St. George in Clarksdale, Mississippi for fourteen years.

Suddenly liberated from both the crushing boredom of the International Shoe Company warehouse and the tyranny and pathology of his parents, Tom started the summer in Memphis early. In a letter from Memphis dated May 18, 1935, to Josephine

Winslow Johnson, a woman he knew from the Writers Guild in St. Louis who had just won the Pulitzer Prize for her novel, *Now in November*, Williams describes his health and the new surroundings: "Now that I feel more settled inside, I'll probably start writing my head off again. There're so many fascinating things to write about down here. You should visit these plantations! Everyone down here seems to have a history that you could write volumes about."

The first of two fortuitous Memphis meetings that summer was with Bernice Dorothy Shapiro, a young, unmarried schoolteacher who was an active member of a local amateur theater group called alternately the Garden Players and the Rose Arbor Players. In the middle of a June 25, 1935, letter to his brother Dakin, Williams made it clear that he had made a connection with Dorothy Shapiro and that they were rehearsing for a production of "their" play. With the phrase, "As you know . . . ," the letter is apparently a continuation of an ongoing progress report concerning the Shapiro/Williams play. Recalling the play forty years later in his *Memoirs*, Williams feels more at ease and refers to "Miss Shapiro" as Bernice Dorothy—though he misremembers the year of his 1935 stay in Memphis:

> In that summer of 1934, when I first became a playwright, there lived next door to my grandparents in Memphis, a family of Jews with a very warmhearted and actively disposed daughter named Bernice Dorothy Shapiro. She was a member of a little dramatic club in Memphis. Their productions took place on the great sloping lawn of a lady named Mrs. Roseborough, which accounts for the "Rose Arbor" name of that cry of players. Dorothy wanted me to collaborate with her on a play for the group—she knew that I was a writer and she wasn't. I wrote a play called *Cairo, Shanghai, Bombay!*—a farcical but rather touching little comedy about two sailors on a date with a couple of "light ladies." Bernice Dorothy Shapiro wrote a quite unnecessary and, I must confess, undistinguished prologue to the play.

> Thank God the prologue was short: that's all I can remember in its favor.
>
> The play was produced late that summer. It was not long, either, but it was a great success for the group. On the program I was identified as the collaborator and was given second billing to Dorothy. [2]

And even though the play might be a somewhat confused hybrid, Williams would also record in his *Memoirs* his awareness of what that first production had meant to him: "Still, the laughter, genuine and loud, at the comedy I had written enchanted me. Then and there the theatre and I found each other for better or for worse. I know it's the only thing that saved my life."

* * *

The second major event of that Memphis summer was when Tom Williams began writing his first full-length play, *Candles to the Sun*, which was also to be his first produced full-length play. One of the unusual things about *Candles to the Sun* is that it was possibly co-authored. Another would-be playwright handed his play over to Williams, telling him that he was tired of working on it, and—in effect—saying, "Do what you want with it!" Williams did and eventually turned it into *Candles to the Sun*.

The would-be playwright in question was Joseph Phelan Hollifield, and he is first identified in an August 17, 1935, letter in which Williams describes to his mother all his recent doings in Memphis. Somewhere in the middle, as though the name were already known and required no introduction, Tom abruptly states: "Last two week-ends Mr. Hollifield has taken grandfather and myself to Maywood Mississippi where there is a fine artesian pool. The sun and fresh air have helped me tremendously."[3]

There is but one known letter that Hollifield wrote to Tom Williams: and it is invaluable for what it tells us. It is reproduced here in its entirety:

1159 North Parkway, November 7th.

Dear Tom,

I was very glad to get your letter because I had been wanting to hear from you. The play contest sounds very interesting, I just hope you will be able to do something with The Lamp. It is the only thing I have ever done that I feel is worth anything at all. Whatever you do with it will be all right, I am sure.

Your letter happened to catch me at a very busy time, so I am not going to try to write a letter now, but I am going to write you later. I will send you some material on mining people in Alabama if I can find any. If there is anything that you would like to know before then that I can tell you, please let me know.

Congratulations on getting a story accepted. You see, this is a good place to write. You must come back for some more successful work. I would like to read that story.

Good luck to you with the play.

Your friend,
(autograph signature)
J.P. Hollifield[4]

In the largest sense, this letter—failing any document to the contrary—might serve as a deed of gift, Hollifield's written testimony that he had, willingly and happily, given Tom Williams his play about the coal fields of Alabama, "The Lamp," to do with it whatever Mr. Williams saw fit. "Whatever you do with it will be all right, I'm sure." Hollifield makes it very clear that he is presently busy with other matters. He remains a man of some mystery, a courtly benevolent Gatsby, the subject of a search just begun.[5] No other direct communication between the two is known.

Yet there remain two other items—one is tempted to call them *exhibits*—that must be considered, one of them invaluable to this inquiry into the question of co-authorship: What precisely did each party contribute? The first item is a letter from Williams to his grandfather, worth noting if only because references to Hollifield are so rare. This letter is dated, but the fourth digit of the year date is smudged over and unreadable: Sept. 15, 193?." However, internal evidence proves that 1936 is the year. [6]

The mention of Hollifield comes just before Williams signs off: "If you see Hollifield tell him I am still working on the coal miner play and expect to submit it in the Little Theater Contest this year. I want to visit some real coal mines in Illinois before I do." This confirms that his grandfather was the connection to Hollifield, and further suggests that Williams had not been in touch with Hollifield since the latter's November 7 letter cited above. It seems that Williams never realized his intention to visit coal mines in Illinois.

The second item of paramount interest is the typed title page and text of a play that later would be retitled *Candles to the Sun*. The title page itself reads as follows: *THE LAMP* / (A Drama of the Southern Coal Fields) / by Joseph Phelan Hollifield / and / Thomas Lanier Williams. Here, the title of Hollifield's one-act, "The Lamp," has been retained by Williams after he has taken over, rewritten, and turned it into a full-length play.

With regard to who wrote what in this full-length version, Williams scribbled a clarifying note with a thick dull pencil that spreads down the title page: "Hollifield finished the original one-act play from which the title and partly the idea for this play was derived. I am doing the writing on the present manuscript and he is contributing some material from Alabama. This is just the first draft in very sketchy form—the main theme—sacrifice of individual to *social* ends—is brought out in the final scene. I want to get your opinion before I give any more time to it this summer as I'm not sure it will 'go.'" This note is at least confirmation that the idea for what was to become *Candles to the Sun* came from Joseph Hollifield. Whether or not any of Hollifield's writing remained in the text as it was performed in 1936 has yet to be established though an examination of this and the various extant drafts suggests that Tom Williams wrote or rewrote all of the dialogue.

Williams continued to work on "the coal miner play," and turned out three early versions of *Candles* under different titles that are briefly described following the text of the play. Surely the winning of the play contest by Thomas Lanier Williams for *The Magic Tower* was announced in the local papers, even before its October, 1936, production. Willard Holland, a highly respected local director of a devoted company of spirited St. Louis amateur actors called the Mummers, contacted Williams, whom he had never met, in early September to ask him to write a few scenes, sketches really, to be produced as a curtain-raiser before an Armistice Day presentation of Irwin Shaw's powerful and highly-praised anti-war one-act, *Bury the Dead*. By October of 1936, Tom reports in his journal that "Willard Holland just called up. Wants to see me tomorrow. He has read my long play...." And even though Williams thought his prologue to *Bury the Dead*, titled *Headlines* and produced in November, was "rather botched," his faith in Holland continued and by early 1937, Tom was doing rewrites at Holland's house and confiding to his journal, "He is a master. Could get work out of an oyster."

* * *

Despite its uncertain beginnings, *Candles to the Sun* is an impressive piece of writing, which is all the more remarkable when it is recalled that for poet and short-story writer Thomas Lanier Williams, this was his first try at writing anything full-length for the theater. Colvin McPherson of the *St. Louis Post-Dispatch* (later a supportive friend of Williams') described *Candles* (after its opening on Thursday, March 19, 1937) as one of the strongest plays the Mummers had ever attempted, lauded it as a drama of social content, and praised the writing of this theater novice: "His writing is rarely unsteady and his play has an emotional unity and robustness. It stands on its own feet. Its characters are genuine, its dialogue of a type that must have been uttered in the author's presence, its appeal in the theater widespread."[7]

Set in the Red Hills coal fields of Alabama during the

Thirties, *Candles* deals directly with the pathos of impoverishment due to exploitive working conditions. But it is not simply a period "Labor melodrama," the generic label one reader used to describe it in a reader's report for a Theatre Guild play contest. *Candles to the Sun* is in fact an engaging drama with tragic elements. And while the play is intensely concerned with labor problems and a miner's strike (at one point miners rush out of a meeting and into the living room of a grieving family, crying "Strike! Strike! Strike!"), *Candles* is most concerned with how a set of desperate characters try to work out the problems of their lives. And when we learn in the last scene of *Candles* that the strike has been settled, the playwright leaves us in the dark with regard to the exact terms of settlement, a matter that any true "labor play" would be quick not only to reveal, but also elaborate with instructive dialogue. Williams is more concerned with what will happen next to his major characters than the general issue of labor conditions.

Part of the strength of this work is in the sense that the coal mine is always there as a brooding omnipresence undergirding this small world, dominating the lives of the families whose men work deep below the earth. Suffice it to say, Williams designed a play in which we see life in the mines through three generations of one family, the Pilchers, living in a "mining camp"—neither town nor village, but rather a place where there are virtually no other jobs, only the mine and a company store; where the microcosm of family represents the macrocosm of a suffering community of workers in a company town.

As the action of *Candles* moves toward resolution Fern gives her blessing for the money she has saved for her son's education—for his escape from the mines and their only hope to break the cycle of poverty—to go instead to the union organizer, Alabama Red, so that food can be purchased for the starving miners and their families during the continuing strike. Angry at her sister-in-law's decision, Star asks Red sarcastically, "Oh, she saw the light, huh?"—Red latches on to this popular expression for revelation and spins it into a metaphor that uses the miner's experience of going from the dark underground into the blinding brightness of the sunlit world; this becomes an epistemological metaphor for the problems of perception and cognition—and finally for profound understanding. The metaphor captured in the play's title is also a perfect description of a mystical experience, and at the same time a recapitulation of the miner's daily experience: from light to darkness and back again to light.

And it also goes all the way back to Plato's cave in *The Republic,* with the clear implication of how little of the real reality we truly see: only the merest light slipping down from the upper world of truth and real illumination.

* * *

1 Edwina Dakin Williams [as told to Lucy Freeman], *Remember Me to Tom* (New York: Putnam, 1963) pp. 62-63.

2 Tennessee Williams, *Memoirs* (New York: Doubleday, 1975), p. 41.

3 Albert J. Devlin, Nancy Tischler, editors, *The Selected Letters of Tennessee Williams, Volume I* (New Directions, New York, 2000) pp. 78-9.

4 from the Harvard Theater Collection.

5 The question of a year date for this letter is easily determined, thanks to the last paragraph where Hollifield offers Tom hearty congratulations "for getting a story accepted." Between 1933 and 1938, Williams had only one story published, "Twenty-seven Wagons Full of Cotton," in 1936, and accepted in 1935 as documented in Lyle Leverich's biography of Williams, *Tom, The Unknown Tennessee Williams*, pp. 58 and 607, which establishes 1935 as the missing year date of Hollifield's November 7 letter to Williams.

6 At the beginning of paragraph four of the Sept. 15 letter, Tom mentions that the Webster Groves Theater Guild is beginning to work on his play, *The Magic Tower*, which took first prize in a one-act play contest and was performed on October 13, 1936.

7 Lyle Leverich, *Tom, The Unknown Tennessee Williams* (New York: Crown, 1995) p. 208.

A PERSONAL NOTE FROM THE EDITOR

How a copy of the production script of Tennessee Williams' first produced full-length play, *Candles to the Sun*, came my way in 1989 is an instance of fortuitous happenstance. At the end of the summer of 1989, during a brief stay in Chicago, where I grew up and attended the University of Chicago, I stayed with old friends in order to spend a day or two at the Goodman Theater and the Chicago Public Library looking at early versions of Williams' last produced full-length play, *A House Not Meant to Stand*. There I got to know the Goodman dramaturg, Abbot Crissman. Just before I left the city, Abbot phoned to tell me that a woman named Jane Garrett Carter had called, claiming to have portrayed Tennessee Williams' first heroine in his first produced play, and she wanted to make a copy of that as yet unpublished play, *Candles to the Sun,* for someone who cared to have one. Apparently she had tried the local critics, who showed no interest, and then called the Goodman where she was referred to Crissman. He referred her to me. I told her just before leaving the city that I would write or call her from Ashland, Oregon, where I was going to live and work for a time. She sent the script on a few weeks after my arrival. I was fascinated by a text that I had only glanced at during a first hectic week-long 1984 visit to the Harry Ransom Humanities Research Center in Austin, Texas, where Williams' earliest manuscripts had been deposited in 1962 after being rescued by bibliographer Andreas Brown, now the owner and proprietor of the famed Gotham Bookmart in New York.

Jane Garrett played Williams' first female lead—creating the role of Star, the rebellious daughter of the Pilcher family—and we developed a friendship over the telephone and through the mail. Therefore I would like to dedicate my work on this first publication of *Candles* with respect, gratitude, and affection to Jane Garrett Carter.

—Dan Isaac,
June 2004

PRODUCTION NOTES AND CREDITS

The action of the play takes place in a mining camp in the Red Hill section of Alabama and covers a period of about ten years.

Characters in this reading text:

BRAM
HESTER
FERN
LUKE
JOEL
STARMINERS
BIRMINGHAM RED
TIM ADAMS
MRS. ABBEY
SEAN O'CONNOR
ETHEL SUNTER
MISS SIMPSON
TERRORISTS
MINERS
MINERS' WIVES

Candles to the Sun, by Thomas Lanier Williams, was first produced on March 18th and 20th 1937 by The Mummers of St. Louis, directed by Willard H. Holland, with the following cast:

Bram Pilcher	Wesley Gore
Hester	Genevieve Albers
Star	Jane Garrett
Joel (as a boy)	Donald Smith
Mary Wallace	Jean Fischer
Tim Adams	Al Hohengarten
Fern	Viola Perle
Luke (as a boy)	Lewis Turner
Mrs. Abbey	Mae Novotny

Ethel Sunter	Mary Hoehnberger
Luke	Sam Halley, Jr.
Birmingham Red	Willard Holland
Joel	Gene Durnin
Whitey Sunter	Fred Birkicht
Sean O'Conner	Frank Novotny
1st Miner	Leland Brewer
2nd Miner	Ralph Johanning
3rd Miner	George Drosten
Terrorist Leader	Joseph Giarraffa
Miners' Wives	Lucile Williamson, Ann Bono, Irene Wisdom, Lillian Byrd

Other Miners, Women and a Gang of Terrorists

Scene: the play takes place in a mining camp in the Red Hill section of Alabama.

Scene 1. Bram Pilcher's cabin, early morning.
Scene 2. The same, evening of the next day.
Scene 3. The same, five years later in early summer.
Scene 4. Star's cabin, five years later.
Scene 5. Bram's cabin, a few months later.
Scene 6. The same. Late that afternoon.
Scene 7. The same. That evening.
Scene 8. Star's cabin, two nights later.
Scene 9. The same, immediately following.
Scene 10. Bram's cabin, some weeks later.

Candles to the Sun

SCENE ONE

Scene: Bram Pilcher's cabin. Early morning.

In a mining camp in the Red Hill section of Alabama, it is a typical miner's cabin, sparsely furnished, and dark, lit only by a faint streak of lamplight coming from a partially opened door of an adjoining room.

Bram, a huge shambling figure, barges out of the door and comes stumbling into the room, lunging forward, kicking against furniture and muttering under his breath.

BRAM: Whyncha turn the lamp on? Caint see a dern thing in here. [*There is a loud impact.*] Christ!

HESTER: Whaja do now?

BRAM: Stubbed my toe, by Jesus.

HESTER: Oughter be more keerful. The way you go bargin' around like nothin' human.

BRAM: Wyncha turn the lamp on in the mornins?

HESTER: Turn it on yerself. I got plenty to do. Should think you'd be uster feelin' yer way around in the dark by now anyhow.

BRAM: Where's the lamp at? Here. Got no matches!

HESTER: What?

BRAM: Matches!

HESTER: There's one right on the base.

BRAM [*lighting the lamp*]: There now. Light! [*He looks slowly around him, blinking his eyes, a dull, phlegmatic interest flicker-*

ing on his face. His attention focuses again on the lamp.] Kind of low on oil, Hester.

HESTER: Fill 'er up. You'll find the can settin' next to the coal bucket.

BRAM [*shambling over*]: Hadn't oughter leave coal oil round a stove. Mought start up a fire some night. Burn us all up in our beds. [*He approaches everything, even an oil can, with an air of slow inevitability, almost like a clockwork figure.*]

HESTER: It ain't by the stove. It's in the coal bucket.

BRAM [*filling up the lamp*]: Well, the coal bucket's settin' right by the stove.

HESTER [*her voice rising with irritation*]: Settin' on the other side of the coal bucket from the stove. I reckon I know 'cause I put it there.

BRAM: She's settin' right smack up against the leg of the stove. Ain't even by the coal bucket.

HESTER: Well, someone elst musta pushed it over there. Besides what diff'rince it make long as the fire caint tech it? [*She comes swishing in with a steaming bowl of mush which she claps down on the bare table.*]

BRAM: Might have combustion or somethin'.

HESTER: I'll combustion you if you don't leave off that grumblin'. Set down here and eat yer mush while it's hot. [*She walks over and opens the outside door and then comes back to the table.*]

BRAM: Mush agin?

HESTER: You kin think of more diff'rent things to pester a body with. Spare that milk. It's all we got. [*She stares at Bram with a critical frown as he approaches the lamplight.*] Look at yer Bram. Yer pants ain't buttoned. [*He buttons them.*] When was the last time you had a good shave?

BRAM [*lurching into the chair*]: Shaved Sunday.

HESTER: Yer a holy sight. It's a good thing you don't work out where folks kin see yuh.

BRAM: Unh. Coffee done?

HESTER: Terackly.

[*Bram turns up the lamp, pours milk, etc.*]

BRAM: Bring in more milk with you. This here's all gone.

HESTER [*sharply*]: That whole pitcher?

BRAM: Uh-huh.

HESTER: I told you to spare it. It's all we got. [*She passes off-stage.*] If you're gonna lap up milk like that you'd better buy me a cow.

BRAM: Buy you a cow?

[*This amuses him. He laughs for several moments deep in his chest, then begins voraciously eating mush, bending low over the plate, slobbering. Coming to the bottom, he raises the bowl to his mouth and drinks the remainder. He wipes his mouth on the back of his hand and begins to stamp his feet under the table.*]

HESTER [*with shrill anger*]: Quit that stompin'!

BRAM [*continuing to stomp*]: Git muh coffee in here.

HESTER: You quit that stompin' or I'll empty the pot on your head!

BRAM: Git it in here. S'bout time for the whistle.

HESTER [*bustling in with coffee pot and tin cup*]: You'll have to drink it black.

BRAM: No cream?

HESTER: Not a drap.

BRAM: Hunh.

[*Hester fills his cup. He instantly starts to raise it to his mouth.*]

HESTER [*grabbing his hand*]: Don't drink it now. It's scaldin'. [*She notices the lamp which he has turned too high.*] Bram. [*She turns it way down.*]

BRAM: Leave it be.

HESTER: You got it turned way too high. [*She dusts off the base with her apron.*]

BRAM: I like it turned high. It makes a good light.

HESTER: It's a waste o' coal oil. You kin see plenty with it turned half that high.

BRAM: Caint see now.

HESTER: You're gittin' blind as a bat.

BRAM [*almost in a bellow*]: SUGAR!

HESTER [*slamming it on the table*]: Quit that hollering. Here.

[*She starts to exit. Bram burns his mouth on the coffee and utters a loud yell.*]

HESTER [*returning to the kitchen*]: There you go. I toleja it was scaldin'. Why don't you listen. [*She hurries out.*]

BRAM: For Chrissake gimme some water!

HESTER [*fetching a dipper of water*]: Not so loud! You'll wake the kids up.

BRAM: Water, water, water!

HESTER: Aw shut up! I toleja the coffee was hot. You just don't listen. Not so loud, now. Star and Joel's asleep.

BRAM: Ohh. Asleep, huh. What of it? They ought be up by now. Layin' in bed's a bad habit. That Joel, he gits lazier ev'ry day of his life. If he don't git to work before long he won't be fit fer nothin'.

HESTER: Joel's goin' to school. You know that.

BRAM: What good does school do a coal miner I'd liketa know.

HESTER: Joel ain't a coal miner.

BRAM: He's gonna be though. Everybody's coal miners round here.

HESTER: I got somethin' else in mind for the boy.

BRAM: Yes, like you had for John.

[*There is a pause. Hester seats herself with her own tin cup, but does not drink. There is a tense brooding look on her face.*]

BRAM: Sent him off an he never come back an you never heerd tell of the boy enny more.

HESTER: Quit harpin' on that. John's all right.

BRAM: You got no idea what become of John. I ain't neither. He shoulda stayed here. Abbey woulda put him on with me. Then you'd been knowin' where he was right now stead of gittin' them advertisements put in the Birmingham paper. Lot a good them done you with John no more able to spell out his own name than you are yours. [*He laughs grimly.*]

HESTER [*with sudden force*]: Joel's gonna git him an eddication.

BRAM: Hunh.

HESTER: Withouten that he'd never be nothin' but what you are.

BRAM: Ain't that good enough? [*Hester groans.*] The company never shoulda put up that schoolhouse. I was aginst it then and I'm still aginst it.

HESTER: The company wouldn't a put it up if the state hadn't forced 'em to. They'd rather we stay as iggerunt as a litter o' pigs round here. It makes us easier for them to make use of.

BRAM: Well, we got no use fer a schoolhouse. They was right about that. It costs us money to keep the dern thing a-runnin' an that's all it ever done's fur as I kin see. Ceptin' it puts a lot o' fool notions in the minds of the young-uns and gives 'em the idea they're too good fer their own folks.

HESTER: Sure. That's the way you look at it. You're what I'd call a natcheral born slave.

BRAM: What d'ya mean by that?

HESTER: I mean you don't know what it is to be free or even want to be free. The mines have you hawg tied and you don't even care. Why, if they was to shut down the mines tomorrer, where'd you be?

BRAM: The mines won't shut down. Long as there's coal in the Red Hills there'll be us miners diggin' it out.

HESTER: In Wes' Virginny the mines shut down fer eight months.

BRAM: Who's been tellin' you all this stuff anyhow?

HESTER: Miss Wallace told me.

BRAM: Who's she?

HESTER: She's the new school teacher.

BRAM: Well, why don't she teach school an keep her nose out of other folks' business. [*He shoves cup toward Hester.*] Gimme 'nother cup coffee.

HESTER: If you don't quit drinkin' so much I'll have to start usin' chicory.

BRAM: Gimme full cup.

HESTER: That's all you git. I'm savin' the rest for Joel. You drank up all the milk. [*She sits down again.*] Miss Wallace says Joel's right quick at his books. Of course he got an awful late start, but he's already up to the second reader. She says maybe by the time he gits old enough to go the company'll be forced to put up a high school too.

BRAM: That won't never happen long as I'm here to stop it. I guess I got a say about that. When I was Joel's age I was diggin' out coal.

HESTER: And you still are.

BRAM: Damn right I still am, and I will be til the day I die so help me. You won't catch me dependin' on nobody else for the bread I eat.

HESTER: You're dependin' right now on the company for every crumb of bread that goes in your mouth. God knows what you'd do for bread if I didn't bake it myself. It's a caution the price of it down at that store. Thirteen cents for a loaf of bread now. Ethel Sunter says in Birmingham you kin git the same size loaf for seven.

BRAM: We got no place else to trade.

HESTER: Yeah, that's it. Just because they know we ain't got no place else to trade they smack on any kind of price they feel like. That's what I mean by your slavery, Bram. The company runs everything around here and you got to take what they give you and like it.

BRAM [*in the manner of one propounding a great philosophic truth*]: It's dawg eat dawg. That's life fer yuh. Dawg eat dawg.

HESTER: Yeah an it's the underdog that gits eaten. That's why my kids're gonna come out on top. I had hopes for you once, Bram. When we got married I thought you was just stayin' down here in the mines till times got better, but now you been down there twin'y four, twin'-five years an it's still just the same. You don't even wanta git out. And now already they call you "The Old Man of the Mines." Yeah, that's what all of them call you now. "The Old Man of the Mines." Mrs. Abbey the superintendent's wife was tellin' me so yesttiddy at the store like as a compliment, but I seen how she meant it.

BRAM: I ain't ashamed of 'em callin' me that. Them young fellers look up to me, I'm the leader.

HESTER: Why dontcha do somethin' to help 'em git some good outa life?

BRAM: Minin's not bad work. Good times it pays good money. When I was Joel's age me and muh pap was loading sixteen cars between us evry blessed day an' in them days it was real money, seventy cents a ton it was and them mules could draw damn near as much coal as these here enjins kin now. Between us, me and muh pap, we made as much as four, five dollars a day.

HESTER: Things've slumped considerable since then.

BRAM [*somewhat glumly*]: You kin still make a livin'.

HESTER: I wouldn't call it a livin'.

BRAM: You eat, dontcha?

HESTER: Not much. After you and the kids git finished many's the time I have to fill up on water.

BRAM: It's a livin' though.

HESTER: For my sons I want somethin' better than that.

BRAM: What else could Joel do 'round here?

HESTER: How many times do I got to tell you Joel ain't gonna stay 'round here? Him nor Star neither. They're both gonna git outa this place.

BRAM: You want 'em to go off like John done an' never be heard of agin? [*He fills his pipe again.*]

HESTER: Quit harpin' on John.

BRAM: He mought be dead for all you know.

HESTER [*fiercely*]: Don't say things to me like that. It goes right through me like a knife. [*She gets up and looks out the window.*]

BRAM: I'm not sayin' he's dead. I'm just sayin' that seven year 's a long time to go without seein' hide nor hair, nor hearin' a word tell o' the boy. If he'd a stayed here you'd a known where he was.

HESTER: Yes, I'd a known where he was, just as if he'd had a little white cross stuck over his grave, I'd a known where he was. Down there in the ground. I caint see it makes much diff'rence whether you dig in the ground or just lie in the ground, ceptin' one would be I should think a sight more restful than the other. John, he was a smart boy. He wanted to work out on top. He didn't want to be an underground rat like you all his life.

BRAM [*wrathfully*]: So that's what you call me, an underground rat, for makin' you a livin' all these years. [*Hester covers her face with her hands.*] Whatsamatter with you anyhow? You been actin' like you was out of your head the last two three days.

HESTER: Maybe I am outa my head. It wouldn't be no wonder if I was. I got somethin' here I didn't tell you about. [*She comes toward him.*] Weighed on me like a rock ever since I got it. [*She draws a letter from her blouse.*]

BRAM: What's that?

HESTER: It's a letter.

BRAM [*taking the letter and turning it curiously in his hands*]: Hmm . . . that's what it is. Who could it be frum you guess?

HESTER: I don't know. But it's got me scared outa my wits. Tim Adams give it to me Thursday mawnin' at the store . . . I started to ask him to read it fer me. He said it come frum Pennsylvainy. But somethin' stopped me. I dunno what. I didn't have the heart to hear it read. Somethin' told me that there was somethin' wrong.

BRAM: John, huh?

HESTER [*slowly*]: Yes, John. He mought be up there. I dunno. Something mought've happened.

BRAM: Git Star to read it. She ought to be able to read by now.

HESTER: No, leave Star be.

BRAM: I'll git her up. [*He starts to the door.*] She'll read it an' then you'll have it off your mind.

HESTER: No, no. Leave her be. She just got in two hours ago. She needs her sleep . . . besides I don't want to read it right now.

BRAM: Got in two hours ago! What dya mean by that? Where she been all that time?

HESTER: I toleja last night that Star was gone to Birmingham for the day.

BRAM: You told me nothin' last night.

HESTER: Then it musta slipped my mind. That letter's been all I kin think of since I got it.

BRAM [*growing excited*]: Where's Star been? You tell me. How come she got in so late? Did she stay out all night?

HESTER: Don't yell at me like that. Star's been visitin' in Birmin'ham with some rich girls she met there. They give her swell presents and take her out on parties and things.

BRAM: Rich girls, huh?

HESTER: They even promised they'd git her a job. Let her be, Bram let her be.

[*Bram has gone into the bedroom and drags Star out by the wrists. She breaks away from him and runs across the room, where she stands sullenly defiant. She is a handsome, mature girl of about sixteen. She wears a red silk kimono.*]

STAR [*looking from one to the other*]: What's all this 'bout I'd liketa know. Draggin' me outa bed like that. Who the holy hell do you think you are?

BRAM [*fiercely*]: Usin' cuss words like any cheap floozie. There's your daughter for you. There she is. Look at her will ya! Who give you that thing you got on! [*Star says nothing but draws it tighter around her.*] WHO GIVE IT TO YOU I SAID. [*He grabs her arm and twists it.*]

STAR: Leggo of me, damn you. It's none of your business.

HESTER: Ain't I toleja Bram it was girls in Birmingham, rich society people that give her them things?

BRAM: Don't give me that stuff. Maybe I am an underground rat, but I still got sense enough in my head to know that it weren't no Birmingham girls that give her them cathouse rags she's got on. Who was it, huh? Who give you them things?

STAR: Leave me be. [*She jerks away from him.*] What did you ever give me that you should make such a fuss!

BRAM: The bread you eat, that's what I give. Now I'll give you something more if you want it. [*He slaps her.*] I'll give you that!

STAR [*gasping*]: You can't do that. You can't pull stuff like that on me. You goddam ole fool you. I guess I gotta have friends all right.

BRAM: You gotta have friends have you.

STAR: Sure I have and places to go.

BRAM: Then go to them.

HESTER: Bram, you can't do that. It's craziness. [*To Star.*] Honey, you can't listen to that man. He's out of his head. [*To Bram.*] Yes, Bram you get to listen. Star ain't done a thing wrong, I swear that she ain't. Your own daughter, Bram, you know better than to think such a thing . . . [*She gasps and covers her face.*]

STAR [*harshly*]: Maybe he's right. Yeah. Maybe it ain't no rich girls that give me these things. What of it? I'm young. I want some fun out of life. I'll tell you who took me to Birmingham. Jake

Walland did . . . [*Hester gasps as though struck.*] It was him that bought me the hat and the shoes and the new pocketbook. Yeah, and he bought me this. He bought me everything that I brung home with me. What of it? We had a swell time. [*She laughs wildly.*] Sure we did, we had a swell time in Birmin'ham, me and Jake Walland did . . . and if you think that I'm sorry . . . .

HESTER [*slowly, stunned*]: No, no, it ain't true.

BRAM: She went with Jack Walland! Did you hear? [*He comes toward Star threateningly.*] You went with that dirty skirt-chasing . . . .

HESTER: Bram!

BRAM: You let him . . . .

HESTER: Bram!

BRAM: Git outa here, you dirty little . . . .

STAR: Sure I'll go. I got places to go all right. Places right here in this camp I can go.

HESTER: Star, don't go. For God's sake, Star don't go. [*To Bram.*] You got to stop her, Bram. She can't go off like this—to that man! [*Star darts out the cabin door. Hester starts to follow her, then rushes to Bram and clutches her arm.*] Stop her, Bram. She can't go like that. Bring her back.

BRAM: No, let her go with him . . . I'm through.

[*He goes out slowly and slams the door. Hester opens the door and stands there with her back to the audience. Joel, a small boy of about eleven, appears in the inner doorway.*]

JOEL [*frightened*]: Mom, what's the matter?

HESTER [*turning slowly, dazed*]: Nothing. Nothing, Joel. [*Her eyes begin to focus on him.*] Git dressed, Joel, and go on to school and study hard as you kin. Your mama's not feeling good.

JOEL: Was something wrong in here just now? Look, Mama, you dropped something on the floor. [*It is the letter. Joel hands it to his mother. She turns it dully in her hands.*] What is it, Mama? Is it a letter? [*Hester says nothing, but stands there dully.*] Why dontcha turn the lamp out, Mama! It's daylight now.

HESTER: Yes, the lamp, turn it out. And take the letter to school with you and git your teacher to read it and let you know what it says.

[*Joel takes the letter from her hand. Extinguishes lamp and goes quietly into the inner room.*]

HESTER [*brooding to herself*]: I think—John's dead . . . .

[*She picks up Star's red silk belt and folds it slowly around her fingers.*]

CURTAIN

SCENE TWO

Scene: Bram's cabin. Evening of the next day.

The schoolteacher, Miss Wallace, has just finished reading the letter to Hester and Bram. Bram sits stoically puffing his cob pipe in the chair by the stove. Miss Wallace sits in the armchair by the small lamp table. Hester paces distractedly about the room, touching things absently with her nervous hands. Joel crouches timidly on the floor in one corner. Miss Wallace is a youngish, fluttery person in a neat tailored suit and dark hat.

BRAM: Seems like she should been here before now. Said she was aleavin' when she wrote the letter. How long did you keep it, Hester?

HESTER: Three days.

BRAM: Three days. It don't take that long to come from Philadelphia. [*He knocks his pipe on the stove and refills it from a leather pouch.*] Read it over again, willya, Miss Wallace? Seems like I just couldn't take it all in.

HESTER [*in a choked voice*]: I heard all I want. I don't wanta hear no more of it. It goes through me like a knife, every word of it. [*She walks blindly over to the table and places her hands on a large bunch of turnips and carrots, raises the knife to cut them, then lowers it slowly to the table and stands motionless, apparently forgetting what she had started to do.*] Read it to Bram. I gotta get on with supper.

MISS WALLACE: You want me to read the whole thing over again, Mr. Pilcher?

BRAM [*clearing his throat*]: No, just read me that part about him going to work there in them Yankee coal mines. That's what I can't get straight in my head.

HESTER: John hated the coal mines. That was why he left home.

BRAM: Yeah, that was your doin', Hester. You done your best to poison his mind against his own father's occupation. But it was in his blood, you see, just like I toleja. In our family we been diggin' coal fer hunerds o' years. What I caint understand is why he wanted to work up there in them damn Yankee mines in Pennsylvainy. Why didn't he come back down here where he belonged 'stead of workin' up there where they got all them damn fool contraptions like machine loadin' and things to kill people with.

HESTER: John's dead. Don't you understand, Bram. What difference does it make what mines he was workin' in long as he's dead anyhow?

BRAM: Just the same I wish you'd read it over agin, Miss Wallace. It don't come straight in my head. That part about him quittin' the job on the cattle boat and goin' to work in the mines . . . .

MISS WALLACE [*reading*]: "Of course, when John and me got married John had to quit his job on the boat . . . "

HESTER: It was her that made him quit. If she hadn't married him he'd be living now.

MISS WALLACE [*continuing*]: ". . . John tried getting jobs everywhere but work was so scarce and times was so bad. There was nothing he could do it seemed like but work in the coal mines and so that was what it come to, though me and John both hated mining . . . ."

HESTER: *She* hated mining, did she? What did it matter to her what my boy had to do. He was gone from home seven years, Miss Wallace, and we never got a word from him all that time. But just the same I was glad he was gone because I thought he was out of the coal mines. That was what I wanted for John, Miss Wallace, that was what I worked so hard for, to keep him out of the mines. There wasn't no school here when John was a kid so he got no learnin' at all. Couldn't write his own name. Just like Bram. All he known how to do was dig coal. But I was dead set aginst him doing that. I give him all the money I'd saved to take him down to Mobile and buy him the few things he needed. And then he was gone, not a word did we hear from him all that time . . . but still I was glad he was gone 'cause I thought he was out of the mines. Now this here woman she writes me and tells me John's dead. He was killed in the coal mines.

MISS WALLACE: Oh, Mrs. Pilcher. I know how you feel.

BRAM: Don't take on so, Hester, you're gettin' Miss Wallace all upset. I wanta hear the rest of it. I still can't make it all out.

MISS WALLACE: Where was I now? Oh yes . . . "John was ashamed you should know he'd gone back to the mines and that was the reason he never let me write you a letter about us getting married and all. We planned as soon as we got some money saved up we'd go into something else, maybe start a little business or buy a farm somewheres so John could work outdoors like he wanted to and the little boy could grow up to be strong . . . ."

HESTER: The little boy! John's son!

BRAM: Yeah, John's son. At least he's got a boy, Hester. You got that to be thankful for.

HESTER: What did it say the boy's name was?

BRAM: She said it was Luke.

MISS WALLACE: Yes, Luke, a good old Biblical name. It means light.

HESTER: Light!

MISS WALLACE: Yes, that's what it means.

BRAM: Go on with the letter, Miss Wallace.

MISS WALLACE [*continuing to read the letter*]: "But our plans, they never worked out somehow. The company stopped paying cash. Instead they paid us paper money called scrip that you couldn't use anywhere but the company store so we had to buy everything there and prices went up so high it was all we could do to keep living, and then sometimes we couldn't even get any scrip. We got behind on the rent and the company took all John's pay 'cause the house we lived in was theirs. Everything was theirs, it all belonged to the company. And for weeks at a time the mines would be shut down and there wouldn't be food in the house and the rent way behind till it got so we owed so much that we couldn't ever catch up. And then this awful thing happened to John in the mines, he got caught on the tracks and the car . . . ."

HESTER [*almost shrieking*]: No, no, don't read that part over. Excuse me, Miss Wallace, I just couldn't stand to hear it.

BRAM: Well, it should be a lesson to these people that are always wantin' new-fangled contraptions—what do they do? —they git killed on 'em, that's all.

HESTER: Don't Bram! Miss Wallace, excuse me for takin' on like this.

MISS WALLACE [*dabbing her eyes*]: I know how you feel, Mrs. Pilcher. I haven't any children of my own, but believe me, I know how you feel.

HESTER: It's that woman that done it all. Yes. She dragged my boy down in the mines to make her a living and she killed him down there.

BRAM: Now, Hester—

HESTER [*fiercely*]: Yes, she killed him, that's what she's done. Her and the mines together, they killed my boy and now she writes about him as if he'd been all her'n. It was me that give birth to him, wasn't it? It was me that brung him up and worked and sweated over him—it was me, not her!

Oh, I know her kind. I can see it all just as plain as if it had happened right in front of my eyes. Her, the cheap, lazy kind that wears loud perfume and fancy clothes and lays around the house all day while my boy worked his poor life away down there in them dirty black holes!

BRAM: Don't take on like that, Hester. She don't sound like that kind of girl to me. You heard in the letter how they went hungry and the company shut the place down and all they had was this paper stuff called scrip.

HESTER: Oh, she didn't hurt herself none, you can depend on that.

BRAM: I don't see that she was to blame for what happened. John had it in his blood to dig out coal. He couldn't do nothing else anyhow. So why was the girl to blame?

MISS WALLACE: I think Mr. Pilcher's right. The girl must've done the best she could, Mrs. Pilcher. You can tell that from the letter. She must have been simply crushed, poor thing!

HESTER: You needn't feel sorry for her. I know her kind. They bleed the life from one man and then they go on to the next!

Excuse me, Miss Wallace, I just can't seem to get quieted down inside . . . .

BRAM [*clearing his throat*]: Well, Hester—now that her and John's boy are comin' down here to live with us—

HESTER: She ain't comin' here—I tell you that flat.

BRAM: But she says she ain't got no place else to take the boy, Hester.

HESTER: The boy can come—but not her.

BRAM: Her folks are dead.

MISS WALLACE: Yes and she's sick, poor girl.

BRAM: I reckon she ain't got no place else to go.

MISS WALLACE [*fluttering*]: Oh, I should think she should've arrived by now—I do hope nothing's happened to the poor girl. I think it's so unsafe for a woman to travel alone—unprotected—these days! Well, I— [*She starts to get up.*]

HESTER: She's probably got herself a new man by now. That's it. Lord knows what she's done with John's boy.

BRAM: I reckon they'll git here sooner or later.

HESTER: We'll take the boy, Bram, but not her. Not that woman. I just dare her to try to set her foot in this house!

MISS WALLACE: Oh, dear, I—

HESTER: Besides, we got no room for her.

BRAM [*slowly*]: She kin have Star's room.

HESTER [*fiercely*]: What're you talking about? Star's room!

BRAM: Star's gone. She kin have Star's room.

HESTER: Star's coming back. She ain't gone for good.

BRAM: Gone for good or for bad, I'll tell you one thing. She ain't never coming back here. She's took up with that sonova—

HESTER: Bram!

BRAM: Excuse me, Miss Wallace. I forgot you was here. Anyhow, he kin keep her now. I'm through.

MISS WALLACE [*shocked*]: I — I — I really think I'd better be tripping along—the weather's so uncertain—you know how it is, I—I have a slight cold in the chest— [*She opens the outside door, wrapping woolen scarf about her chest. She steps outside, then darts back in with a frightened exclamation.*] Oh, dear, there's a—a *disorderly* couple out there on the street! I'd better wait till they pass— [*Her mouth is agape.*] The woman is so intoxicated she can hardly walk. Why it's—oh, my stars, it's Mr. *Adams*!

BRAM: He's coming up here, I do believe!

MISS WALLACE: Oh, Mr. Adams! You gave me such a fright! Oh, my dear, I—

ADAMS: Good evenin', Miss Wallace. [*He appears in the doorway supporting Fern, who seems barely conscious.*] Got a mighty sick young woman here. Come into my store just now and keeled right over at the counter. Sez she's lookin' for some folks name o' Pilcher so I reckon it must be you. Was you expectin' her Mizz Pilcher?

HESTER [*after a long pause*]: Well, I—

BRAM: Yes, we was expectin' her.

ADAMS: Come on in, young lady. Mighty nasty weather we been having lately. Ole Hetty, my sister, come down agin with the break-bone fever. Seems like ever fall she has a spell of it.
What become of the young man? Had a young man with us a moment ago. Oh, there you be, young feller, skulkin' behind yer mummy's skirt. Come on out here in the light where folks kin take a good look at yer—

HESTER [*darting forward with a smothered cry*]: John's boy! It's John's little boy! The same eyes! [*She snatches off his cap.*] And the same hair! John's hair used to curl like that every time it rained in a thousand or so little rings all over his head! He's John all over again—I swan! [*She turns.*] Bram! Don't stand there like a stick!

BRAM [*stupidly*]: What d'ya want me to do?

HESTER: What do I want him to do, what do I want him to do? I swan, you git more thick in the skull every day!! Bring their things in!

[*Bram exits with Adams.*]

HESTER [*to the boy*]: Come over here, honey, and set yourself down by the stove. You must be wet clean through. [*To Fern.*] I bet you ain't got him a bite to eat all day, huh? I'll fix you a cup of hot tea, that I will, and I'll put you a spot of rum on it.

[*Bram enters with one little bag.*]

BRAM: Here's the girl's things.

HESTER: That all?

BRAM: Want 'em put in Star's room?

HESTER [*caught short*]: Star's room? [*After a pause.*] Star's gone. Yes. I reckon—you mought jist as well put 'em in there.

CURTAIN

Scene: Five years later. Front room of Bram's cabin, a morning early in summer.

Sunlight streaming through the open door and window give the room a much sprightlier appearance than in the preceding scene. Fern is discovered at a big wooden wash-tub in the middle of the floor, full in the stream of sunlight. She's changed—no longer a slight, pathetic figure, she is now a robust and capable-looking woman, dressed in blue calico. She moves purposefully about, as though directed in all she does by a single driving motive. Her face wears a set, determined expression.

After a minute Mrs. Abbey appears at the door. A scrawny affectatious gossip dressed in what she considers the height of style. A woman who obviously lords it over all whom she considers beneath her. She carries a bundle of clothes, which she deposits on the table.

MRS. ABBEY: I brought you another big load of wash. Where's Mrs. Pilcher?

FERN: She gone to the store.

MRS. ABBEY: Oh, yes. Joel's working there now, I see.

FERN: He's clerking there.

MRS. ABBEY: Now isn't that nice! Joel never was a very strong boy so I guess the store is just the place for him— [*She smiles maliciously, seats herself and takes off one of her shoes.*]

FERN: Oh, Joel's strong enough. But Hester just doesn't want him to work in the mines—she—she—she wants him to do other things.

MRS. ABBEY: Other things? Well, well, now isn't that nice? Of course it's sort of hard to understand what an able-bodied man could do around a mining-camp besides working in the mines . . . [*She laughs affectedly.*] These new shoes kind of pinch my feet. You don't mind if I set here and cool them awhile? Do you, Fern? [*She takes off both shoes.*] Oh, now, what was it I wanted to speak to you about? Oh, yes. Those purple silk pyjamas of Mr. Abbey's. They got lost in last week's wash!

FERN [*sharply*]: Lost? In the wash?

MRS. ABBEY: Yes, they wasn't returned. They must've gotten mixed up somehow with some of Mr. Pilcher's things don't you think?

FERN [*stiffly*]: No, they couldn't possibly of gotten mixed up with anything of Bram's. First place, Mrs. Abbey, there wasn't any purple silk pyjamas in the wash last week. There was just two pairs of pink ones and a pair of green ones. There was a pair of purple pyjamas split all to pieces about two weeks ago.

MRS. ABBEY: My, my, I don't see how you can remember!

FERN: I make a list of everything I take out of the bundle. If you want me to I can show it to you.

MRS. ABBEY: Oh, no, that ain't necessary, Fern. If you say so I'll take your word for it. Of course it did seem peekyulyer—the pyjammers being missing like that—but as I was saying to Mr. Abbey—Fern's been doing my wash for five years and I never had no reason yet to suspicion her of any dishonesty. Well, I just wish you'd be a *little* more careful in the future, that's all!

FERN [*with controlled anger*]: I don't see how I could be any more careful than I am, Mrs. Abbey. If you really feel that—that . . . .

MRS. ABBEY: Now, Fern, you know I never thought any such thing. Me and Mr. Abbey have the greatest respect for Mr. and Mrs. Pilcher. Mr. Abbey was saying just the other day that Bram's been with us longer'n any other man in the outfit. They call him "The Old Man of the Mines"! [*She giggles behind her hand.*] Think of that! And he's still such a strong hard worker—of course they do say his eyesight's kind of gone back on him lately—aint it Fern?

FERN: Yes.

MRS. ABBEY: Well, I guess down there in the dark all the time like he is it don't matter much whether he can see so good or not— Well, it's just wonderful they way all the men look up to him and all, ain't it though . . . Oh, I forgot! [*She makes an excited gesture.*] The most peekyulyer thing happened in the store the other day! Did you hear about it?

FERN: No.

MRS. ABBEY: Well—I almost hate to tell you about it, it sounds so—awful! I was just a-callin' for my mail when who should come in the store but that—that sister-in-law of yours—the one that—oh, what's her name?

FERN: You mean Star?

MRS. ABBEY [*tittering*]: Oh, is that what you call her? Mmm. I never know whether to say Miss Pilcher or Mrs.—what's the name of that man who she went to live with, that—Jake person? Well, anyway, in she comes and she walks up to the counter and starts talking to Joel when who should come following her in but that awful red-headed woman who lives in that house cross the tracks—you know—the woman they say all those—horrible things about—well, she comes up to your sister-in-law and she—oh, I just hate to tell it, it sounds so awful—well, she *spits* right in

Star's face! Yes, without saying a word she just comes up and spits right smack in Star's face! Did you ever hear tell of—

FERN: Spit—in Star's face!

MRS. ABBEY: Yes, and that's not all. Your sister-in-law, Star, she wheeled around and slapped her—yes—and then she busted out crying, Star did, and ran on out of the store and the red-headed woman ran after her lickety-split and called her a name. I just wouldn't dare to repeat—I just wouldn't *dare*!— My, my, as I was saying just the other day to Mr. Abbey, I think that red-headed woman ought to be rid out of town on a fence rail. Just imagine her calling a nice young girl like your sister-in-law Star a name like that. Can you understand it? Well, Joel, he runs out after 'em and that leaves just me and Mr. Adams there in the store by ourselves and I was just so flabbergasted I couldn't speak for a minute and then I turns to Mr. Adams and I says, "For Heaven's sake, Mr. Adams, what do you suppose them two women was carryin' on like that about?"—an' he just laughs and winks at me an' says, "Well, I reckon it's just a case of perfessional jealousy." Now what do you suppose he meant by that? Honest, I must be awful dumb but I just couldn't make head or tails of it all!

[*Fern has grimly returned to her washing. Mrs. Abbey rises, smiling with satisfaction, her tale being told.*]

MRS. ABBEY: Well, I really ought to be getting home now. And about those purple pjyammers, Fern, now I . . . .

[*Hester appears in door. She carries a market-basket. She is very old and worn-looking. She glances at Mrs. Abbey and gives her a cold nod, then plumps basket down on the table.*]

MRS. ABBEY [*with renewed excitement*]: Well, well, Mrs. Pilcher, how are you? You look kind of peaked!

HESTER: I'm all right.

MRS. ABBEY: I was just tellin' your daughter-in-law here, the most peekyulyer thing happened the other day that I ever—

FERN [*interrupting sharply*]: Mrs. Abbey, when do you want this wash back?

MRS. ABBEY: Why, the usual time, Fern. Why? Won't you be able to git it done that soon?

FERN: The usual time. Good-bye, Mrs. Abbey.

MRS. ABBEY: OH—oh, yes—goodbye.

[*She moves huffily toward the door, her lips compressed with disappointment at being shut off.*]

MRS. ABBEY: Oh, and as I was saying about those silk pyjammers of Mr. Abbey's, if you should just *happen* to come acrost them in among Bram's or Joel's things—by accident you know . . . .

HESTER [*bristling*]: Silk pyjammers? Among whose things? Mrs. Abbey, I'd like you to know my husband and my son, neither of them, would take anything that belonged to Mr. Abbey or nobody else, so if you're suggestin' anything of that kind—

MRS. ABBEY: My, my, Mrs. Pilcher, you sure have got a quick tongue! [*She draws herself up.*] It seems like some people kind of forget—

HESTER [*trembling with anger*]: No, I ain't forgotten nothing. I know your husband is superintendent and runs these coal mines and I know you un your husband, but when it comes to you walking right in my own house and calling my son or my husband a thief—

FERN [*interceding anxiously*]: Hester, I don't think she meant—

MRS. ABBEY: Never mind, Fern. I'm not takin' offense. Any woman that has the worries on her mind that poor Mrs. Pilcher has, with a daughter like that Star running loose around the camp—

HESTER [*fiercely*]: That's enough outa you! Get outa here now! Get right outa here now! Git right outa this house! And take your dirty wash with you! [*She seizes bundle on table and thrusts it violently into Mrs. Abbey's middle, pushing her toward door with it.*] And your dirty tongue and git outa this house!

MRS. ABBEY: *What*—why, I—*never*!

HESTER: Take it all out with you, your damned silk pyjamas and things and wash 'em yourself. And you can tell your husband I said so and he can do any damned thing he wants to about it. And don't let me ever catch you with the name of my daughter or my son or my husband on your tongue again in this house or any other house, I don't care if your husband runs every coal mine in the State o' Alabama! (*Pause.*) I'm not one of your *slaves*!

MRS. ABBEY [*choking with rage*]: Mr. Abbey will hear about this! He'll be informed how one of his miners' wives had the impertinence to talk to me!

[*She drops some clothes as she flies out the door. Hester grabs the bundle Mrs. Abbey dropped and flings it after her. There is a moment's pause. Then Mrs. Abbey appears at the door again.*]

MRS. ABBEY: I'll trouble you for my shoes! [*She gets them and gets out.*]

FERN [*with mingled fear and admiration*]: Hester! You shouldn't have acted like that.

HESTER: Why not? I've been meek as Moses too long with that woman. It sure did my soul good to let her have it like that. Well, let her tell old man Abbey. He won't fire Bram. He wouldn't have the guts. Why, if Bram got fired half the men in the mines would walk out with him and old man Abbey knows it.

FERN: How about Joel's job at the company store?

HESTER [*struck aghast*]: OH! Oh, *God*! I hadn't thought about that! [*She sinks weakly into a chair.*] She'll get him fired! She'll make Tim Adams fire Joel, won't she?

FERN: More'n likely. Don't worry about it now.

HESTER [*slowly*]: No, it's too late. I've gone and done it. I should've held my tongue. But I'm tired of it, Fern. The reason we've had to eat so much dirt around this camp is because we never had guts enough to th'ow it back in their faces! [*Huskily.*] I'm tired of it, Fern. I'm gittin' old.

FERN: You ain't old yet.

HESTER: Ain't old? I'm as old as those everlastin' hills out there. That's how old I am! [*She laughs bitterly.*] An the devil's gittin' hold of my spirit! [*She rises and her voice becomes excited.*] I'm gonna give 'em back as good as I git frum now on. I don't care what happens. I'm gonna start fightin'. It's time somebody started fightin'. Bram won't, he's too dumb. He's a natcheral bo'n slave. But me, I'm gittin' tired of it all. I've been around here a long time, pretty near my whole life. I've seen 'em live an die in this camp, their whole lives from beginning to end, digging down in the dirt and getting nothing out of it but life enough to keep on digging.

That's all. It's time somebody did something round here besides dig in the dirt and eat it. *I'm fed up*! [*She pants breathlessly, clutching her chest.*]

FERN [*after a slight pause*]: I'm fed up on it too. But gittin' sore at people like Mrs. Abbey don't help us none. It just lost me their washing and Joel his job. I needed that washing. I needed the money.

HESTER: It's time you quit doing people's dirty wash, Fern. You're still young and good lookin'. There's plenty of single men round here who'd be more'n glad to have you cookin' their vittles fur em.

FERN: You tryin' to get shed of me now?

HESTER: I'm givin' you good advice. No use makin' a slave of yourself. Better get some fun outa life while you can. [*She goes into the kitchen.*]

FERN: I'm not lookin' for fun. [*She goes to outside door.*] Luke! Oh, LUKE! [*His voice is heard faintly replying.*] Take the bucket and go down there by the spring and see if you can't find a few blackberries for lunch.

LUKE [*off-stage*]: Okay, Mom. Soon as I finish this page.

FERN: He's still readin'. [*She turns to Hester, who has come back on.*]

HESTER: He likes his books, don't he!

FERN: He reads all the time. Everything he kin lay his hands on. Miss Wallace says he's bright as a dollar.

HESTER: Like John.

FERN: Yes. He's like John was.

HESTER: He's like you, too. He's got your quick, lively ways about him.

FERN: No, he's like John in his ways too. He's just like John and I'm glad of it. It's like John was living agin.

HESTER [*after a pause*]: John was my first son, Fern, and God only knows how it hurt to lose him, but still—I think you should try not to think so much about what's over and done. You got life in front of you still. What's done's done. I remember the day that schoolteacher read us your letter about John's death. I hated you then. I thought somehow it was all your fault, him getting killed in them mines up there. But when you come in that door the first time, an' that awful lost look in your eyes—I know you wasn't to blame for what happened. I see what you felt was even worse than what I felt. But that was a long time ago . . . it's time you started living again, Fern.

FERN [*wringing out a piece of wash*]: I am living again—for John's boy. Everything I do's for him, every cent I can make so's when he's grown a man like John was I can pay it all back to him, what I took from his father.

HESTER: You never took nothing from John.

FERN: If it wasn't for me maybe John would've got what he wanted.

HESTER [*looking at her closely*]: What did John want?

FERN: What you wanted for him and what he wanted for himself and what he never did get because he was married and had to earn a living and didn't have no other way of earning it but digging down in the dirt for it and getting smashed down there.

[*There is a long pause during which Hester busies herself with preparing some vegetables at the table. Fern wanders over to the open window.*]

FERN: Luke's running down the hill to the spring lickety-split. Hear him? He's whooping at the top of his lungs. And beating on the blackberry bucket like it was a drum.

HESTER [*going to the window*]: I can't see. The sun's in my eyes.

FERN: I reckon he must be playing Injun or something.

HESTER: I can't see for the sun. It's too bright.

FERN [*after a moment*]: Now he's running back up. What legs he's got!

HESTER [*excitedly*]: Yes, I kin see him now. He's—oh! [*She turns away from the window and goes slowly to the store, her face drawn into a look of agony.*]

FERN [*her eyes still on the boy*]: He's got to the top now. He's shinning up that big cottonwood tree. Maybe I better call him off. He might fall.

[*She turns toward Hester. Notices her suffering.*]

FERN: Hester, what's the matter with you? You're white as goat milk!

HESTER [*getting up stiffly*]: Nothing's the matter with me.

[*She resumes her work. There is another long pause. Then Hester seems to forget what she is doing. Her hands move slower and slower at their occupation and her eyes take on a dreaming expression.*]

HESTER [*as if to herself*]: John used to run down that same hill on bright summer mornings. It hit me all of a sudden. The warm sweet smell of the grass . . . .

THE CURTAIN FALLS SLOWLY

SCENE FOUR

Scene: Five years later. Front room of Star's cabin.

Star's cabin is in startling contrast to Bram's. The keynote of Bram's was a stark, almost barren simplicity. This room is gaudy and expressive in every detail of Star's own personality. Architecturally it is practically the same as Bram's, but garish drapes, calendar pictures, photos of movie stars, kewpie dolls, fancy silk pillows work a complete transformation. In the back wall are one or two large windows opening on the dusky street. In the right wall—or wherever it will best suit the action—is the front door, opening on another street, the cabin standing at the intersection. Both windows are wide open as the scene begins and Star, gaily dressed for the evening, moves about the room as though flaunting herself to the public view. Crowds are passing around the corner on their way to the Saturday night dance or frolic at the miners' meeting houses. Drunken men shout ribaldries and give catcalls as they pass by the two roads. Shrill-voiced women make caustic commentaries. Star smiles with nervous defiance as she overhears these voices. She lights a cigarette. Sometimes she hums to herself. She has a tense, anticipatory air, as though she were definitely waiting for something to happen—or someone to arrive.

Ethel Sunter enters through the open door. Ethel is a homely spinster of strong but thwarted sex impulses, sublimated into a state of almost constant religious ecstacy. Her acts of charity are not prompted so much by a natural good will as by a sense of Christian duty. She is suspicious of all. She peers inquisitively about the room.

STAR [*disappointed*]: Oh, hello, Ethel.

ETHEL: Good evenin'. [*She picks up some cards from the table and gasps.*] I see you been playin' cards.

STAR: No, that's just an old deck I tell fortunes with.

ETHEL: Fortunes! That's wickedness. Only the Lord can tell what's coming.

STAR: Then I sure wish he'd hurry and tip me off. Now that Jake's dead, I'd kinda like to know what's coming next. Set down.

ETHEL: I can't stay but a minute. I brought you somethin' to eat. Just scraps.

STAR: Thanks. I can use 'em.

ETHEL: I didn't git to the funeral.

STAR: Naw. I noticed you wasn't there Ethel.

ETHEL: It was the first layin' under I missed in this camp in nigh on ten years. You see I heard as how Jake Walland wouldn't even profess belief on his death bed, and under them circumstances I couldn't see my way clear to anticipate in his uh—preferment.

STAR [*languidly*]: Naw, I reckon you couldn't.

ETHEL: Now that he's gone, have you made any plans for your future?

STAR: No.

[*Ether's voice begins to shake with religious excitement.*]

ETHEL: There's time in everybody's life when an opportunity comes to go up— [*She points.*] Or down.

STAR: You mean Heaven? You can count me outa that. I've already put in my reservations at the other end. [*She laughs and lights a cigarette.*]

ETHEL: Now, you're just talking sinful. I guess it's the bad company that you been keeping. I seen that red-headed Jezebel frum acrost the tracks prancin' outa here as I come up the walk. What was she doin' here?

STAR: The same thing you're doin'. Preachin' salvation. Only hers was a house in Birmingham. I told her she could count me outa that, too.

ETHEL: I see. I've always felt there was good in you Star, or I wouldn't—I wouldn't . . . .

STAR: You wouldn't've disgraced yourself by comin' in here.

ETHEL: Hmm. I just wanted to know what you was planning to do with yourself now that Jake's dead. [*Her voice rises.*] There's plenteous redemption in the blood of the lamb! Remember that.

STAR: Yeah.

ETHEL: Just remember. It's a glorious thing to be saved. [*She rises, her fervor reaching an almost hysterical pitch.*] I'll never fergit the time that I first saw the light, and before that time Star, I'd been like you—a sinful woman.

STAR [*more amused than resentful*]: You? Sinful?

ETHEL [*in a confidential whisper*]: Yes. In here. [*She points to her breast.*] I was full of sinful thoughts. At night I couldn't sleep. I lay on my bed an sweated an twisted in shameful temptation. But not since then. And you, Star . . . there never was a woman more sorely tempted and tried then I was. What's possible for me is possible for you too. Just remember that. It's a glorious thing to be saved.

STAR: Yeah. I reckon it must be swell.

ETHEL: Who is that comin' up the walk? Oh, it's Luke. [*She coos.*] I declare he's gettin' that big I half took him for a full-grown man. Good evenin', Luke.

LUKE: Is Star inside?

ETHEL: I just left her. [*Luke enters. He is now a boy of about seventeen, dressed in overalls, carrying some worn-looking books under one arm.*]

STAR: Hello, Luke. Come on in. How's the young student? Eating these days?

LUKE: Hello, Star.

STAR: Is Hester any better?

LUKE: She's about the same. Mom's getting worried about her.

STAR [*after a pause*]: I guess Hester's tired out.

LUKE: Yes, the doctor says she needs to take a long rest.

STAR: What doctor? That company doctor?

LUKE: Sure he's the only one we got around here.

STAR: He's no good. He doesn't know a damned thing. He told me that my man Jake just had a bad cold and that he'd be back shoveling coal inside of a week. Well, just three days after that Jake Walland was dead, laid away in his grave, so if he did go back to shoveling coal there's only one place it could be. I guess that's where you'd expect to find him anyhow. He was the orneriest white man in the world, I reckon. Some ways, though, he was all right. He would done anything in the world I wanted him to.

Yeah, he'd've married me if I'd wanted him to. I didn't wanta git married to Jake. I didn't want to git tied down to no man on this earth, and that's the God's truth. You know that it wasn't because Jake wouldn't have me for his wife like some people say. No, it was just because I wouldn't have him nor nobody else. I wanted my freedom too much for that. There isn't any man on this earth that I'd be willing to hitch myself up with for keeps. I don't know why I'm telling you all this. It's no concern of yours. But I know how people talk. I can hear 'em talk just sittin' here in the evening, I can hear 'em talk as they go by he window. They say some rotten things about me, some of them, but I don't care. I don't regret nothing that I ever done. I never had a chance to do diffrent and that's the God's truth and you know it. Turn the lamp up will ya, Luke. I dunno what I turned it down for. I must be gittin' sort of queer in the head. Benn sittin' here by myself so much since old Jake turned in his checks.

LUKE [*turning up lamp*]: I like to sit in the dark sometimes myself.

STAR: You do, what for?

LUKE: Sometimes you can see things plainer in the dark than you can in the light.

STAR: Yeah? What things for instance?

LUKE: Mostly things I read about.

STAR: You read a lot of things, don't you?

LUKE: Much as I can get hold of around here. Books are pretty scarce. There's a fellow named Birmingham Red has a few he loaned me.

STAR: The guy that's been holding them meetings!

LUKE: Yeah.

STAR: You better stay away from him. He's a troublemaker.

LUKE: He's just tryin' to show us how things are. We been pore-hawgin' along for years now—but we've reached the dead-end. When we was workin' regular no matter how little we got paid there was always enough to eat on. But now with the mines shut down half the time and nobody sure where the next meal's comin' from—things have got to be diff'rent. Red was talkin' to me a few nights ago about something called cooperative commonwealth.

STAR: What's that mean?

LUKE: I ain't sure myself about what the words mean, but I was thinkin' it over in bed after I turned the light out and all of a sudden I got an idea of what it was all about and I jumped out of bed and run over to Red's place and we sat up the rest of the night talking some more. It's funny about that guy. He ain't in it for what he can get out of it like everybody else seems to be. He talks about—society. You know—you and me and everybody else that makes up the whole world. It's too big to understand all at once. It's one of those things that you have to lay in the dark and think about a long time before they begin to sink in.

STAR: It's just a lot of hot air. Tell him you don't fall for that kind of stuff.

LUKE: I do, though, Star. I don't think it's always going to go on like this.

STAR: Maybe when you and me have been dead a couple thousand years things will be different.

LUKE: Red don't think it can come all at once neither. But it's worth working for just the same. It's justice . . . that's what he calls it—the principle of social justice.

STAR: Justice . . . that's just one of them words you find in the dictionary. That Birmingham Red he's a funny sort of guy ain't he? He's got a lot of screwy ideas like that. Justice. Equality. Freedom. I go to hear him talk sometimes. I sit in the front row. But he don't even look at me, he looks right over my head, and it makes me so damn mad I want to throw a brick at him and yell at the top of my voice, or something. I guess even then he wouldn't know I was there. What's the matter with him? Don't he go for women?

LUKE: I guess he's got other things on his mind.

STAR: Someday he'll wake up and find out he's human. Maybe he'll take a look at me then. I'm not so bad to look at. I got my good points and I don't keep 'em all under cover with a man like Birmingham Red.

LUKE: What do you want him for, Star. He ain't your sort is he?

STAR: What do you mean he ain't my sort? He's big, ain't he. I always liked big men.

LUKE: He's got brains.

STAR: Yeah, and I can appreciate brains in a guy as well as anyone else. And I can also appreciate good looks. Birmingham Red's the only guy in this lousy mining camp that I'd walk across the street to spit on.

LUKE: Hester wouldn't like to hear you talk like that, Star.

STAR: Hester don't bother about me no more.

LUKE: Yes, she does. She talks about you all the time.

STAR [*huskily*]: Does she?

LUKE: Yes, 'specially since she's sick. She worries about you.

STAR: Worries about me. What for? I can take care of myself.

LUKE: She don't like to you see you living like this.

STAR: Like what? [*After a pause.*] Yeah, I know what you mean . . .

LUKE: What're you goin' to do now?

STAR: Now?

LUKE: Yes, now that Jake's dead.

STAR: Oh, I dunno.

LUKE: You can't stay on here, can you?

STAR: Rent's paid up til the first.

LUKE: The company'll put you out after that if you can't keep payin' the rent.

STAR: Sure they will.

LUKE: Well, now that Jake's gone—you ought to come back home.

STAR: Home? Bram's house? He run me out of there once. When I was just a kid, sixteen, because I stayed out all night with

Jake Walland and come home with a new silk kimona. He run me out of the house for that, when I was sixteen. I was green as grass then. I didn't know a damned thing. Now I'm twenty-six and pretty wise. I can take care of myself—one way or another I don't need to go whining back to Bram's house. I'd starve first. But I won't starve. You can tell that Bolshevik friend of yourn that if he won't give me a tumble there's others that will. I can pick and choose!

LUKE: There's no use talking to you, Star. [*He crosses downstage near the inner door.*]

STAR: There's no use preaching to me, if that's what you mean. [*Music cue.*] Put your shoes on, Luke, and go down there to the dance. The moon's as big and yellow as a pumpkin tonight.—You're young. Have a good time while you can. Pretty soon old Bram'll be draggin' you down in the coal mines with him.

LUKE [*rising and picking up his books*]: No, he won't. Mom's dead set against me working in the coal mines.

STAR: And Hester was dead set against it for John, too, but he got killed in one of them, didn't he?

LUKE: I won't. I'll tell you something. Mom's been putting by some money out of the washing she takes in to send me to college in Tuscaloosa.

STAR: Poor old Hester, nothing worked out right for her. None of us done like she wanted us to. Now she's dying I guess. Sometimes you wonder what it's all about, this living and dying, don't you?

LUKE: If Hester don't get better—I mean if she should take a turn for the worse— [*Goes to her.*]

STAR: Let me know if she does!

LUKE: Would you come and see her?

STAR: A-course. You come and call for me. I'd go with you. I—I wouldn't want Hester to die without forgiving me.

LUKE: She don't hold nothing against you, Star.

STAR: I know. She's got so she speaks to me sometimes on the street. But there's such a—a look in her eyes—when she sees me—It's just as though she was looking at my dead body! [*She rises and turns her back to Luke.*] So long, Luke.

LUKE: So long— [*He pauses a second and then goes out.*]

[*Star moves to the window. A small crowd of townspeople appear at the rear of the stage, observing Star at her window.*]

WOMAN: Look at 'er.

ANOTHER WOMAN: Brave as brass, ain't she?

A THIRD WOMAN: Ought be ashamed to show her face!

MAN: Hi, there, Star. Better come down to the dance.

ANOTHER MAN: Yeah, come along, Star. You ain't gonna be a widow all yer life.

STAR: I ain't a widow.

MAN: Yer a common-law widder, ain'tcha? [*Loud guffaws.*]

STAR: You're too damned smart.

WOMAN: Didja ever see the likes of that? Come on, Sarah! YOU Sam! What're you lookin' in that window for?

ANOTHER WOMAN: Fixin' to catch herself a new man already!

STAR [*smiling with suppressed excitement*]: Who's that?

RED [*opening door*]: Me.

STAR [*after a slight pause, probably to control herself*]: I knew you was coming.

RED: Did you?

STAR: Yeah, that's why I stayed home from the dance tonight.

RED: Well, that's flattering. What made you expect me tonight?

STAR: It's Saturday night. You might call it playing a hunch. [*There is a long pause.*] Set down. Make yourself comfortable. [*Red seats himself in a straight chair by the table. He appears rather constrained.*] That chair's kin' of hard on your back. Why don't you set on the bed? That's where I set mostly.

RED: Do you?

STAR: Yeah. Mostly.

RED: I feel all right here, thank you.

STAR: Was you brought up in a barn?

RED: What do you mean?

STAR: Ain't you never heard of shutting doors when you come in?

[*Red rises and shuts the door. She rises.*]

RED: The air's so nice tonight I thought maybe you'd want it open. What made you think I was coming here?

STAR: I told you. It's Saturday night. [*She crosses to the table.*]

RED: What's that got to do with me coming here?

STAR: Saturday night's pay night. A lot of the boys come to see me on Saturday night. At least they used to. That was the night Jake Walland went out and got drunk and didn't come home til next morning. . . I guess you know who Jake was?

RED: Yeah, he was the lung case that passed out last week. Did you get any flowers from Gomstock Incorporated? [*He sits on the bed.*]

STAR: The company furnished a coffin.

RED: That's good. At the rate they're turning out corpses it'd pay them to go into the coffin business.

STAR: Jake drank his guts to pieces. I guess that was really what done him in.

RED: Hell! Don't you know what he died of even? It was silicosis!

STAR: What's that? [*She moves toward Red a little.*]

RED: It's a special bonus the company gives their employees for long and faithful service. Like some places hand out a gold watch after so many years—our company deals 'em a pair of rotten lungs. That's what killed your man. You see, when they're blasting down there in the shaft they oughta get the men out first, but that would take more time and trouble than Gomstock Inc. figures that they can afford. They'd rather just—settle for a coffin! Maybe some day they'll learn something about practical economy. Now they figure they can't even afford to pay us money. They're paying us scrip. And with prices so high at the company store, there's damned few getting even enough to eat. Pellagra's about as bad among the women as silicosis is with the men. Bram Pilcher's wife's dying of it now—

STAR: Hester—dying of— ?

RED: You know her?

STAR [*after a pause, her voice low*]: Yeah, my mother.

RED: I'm sorry. I didn't know.

STAR: I known she was dying. I didn't know what of. I guess she's been scrimping herself so's the others would have enough. That's like her. I didn't know she had—pellagra. I thought maybe she was jes tired of living—

RED: Maybe she was. I wouldn't blame her for that. Would you?

STAR: No. I wouldn't blame her. [*Sits beside him on bed.*] I wouldn't blame her for being tired of living. Evuh'thing turned out wrong for her—including me.

RED: What's the matter with you?

STAR [*moving closer and placing a hand on his knee*]: I dunno. S'pose you tell me?

RED [*rising and going back to the straight chair*]: Nothing except your technique.

STAR [*huffily*]: Yeah? What's wrong with my technique!

RED: You're a little bit quick on the uptake.

STAR [*smiling*]: I guess you like them kind of hard to get huh? Well, I am hard to get with mos' men. I jes happens that I have a sort a weakness for boys of your type. Why don't you come down off the platform and give us girls a break! Some of us ain't so bad when you get to know us better. They tell me you go to bed at night with the dictionary. Huh? [*She laughs softly and stretches herself provocatively on the bed.*]

RED: I don't like women who can't talk clean.

STAR [*rising furiously*]: Oh, you big stiff, you give me a pain. What did I say that was dirty I'd liketa know? I didn't know you was a Sunday school teacher.

RED [*still quietly*]: I'm not. But I like my women to talk decent.

STAR: What the hell did you come here for? To talk about the weather? It's a swell night, ain't it? Just like spring!

RED [*after a pause*]: It *is* spring. You can smell the honeysuckle.

STAR [*somewhat pacified*]: Yeah. It *does* smell kind of good at night. [*She goes over and sits down by the window on upper edge of bed.*]

RED: That's a sprig of it you've got pinned on your dress. Isn't it?

STAR: Yeah. I pulled it off one of them vines down there by the spring.

RED [*going over to her*]: Let me smell it. [*He seats himself on the window still beside her and presses his face against her breast.*]

STAR [*pushing away*]: Now *you're* going a little too fast.

RED: Am I? I thought you liked plenty of speed.

STAR: Well, I always slow down on the curves. Go back over and sit in the chair. [*He doesn't move.*] If you caint act like a gentleman you'd better not stay. [*Archly.*] I like to CONVERSE with my gentleman visitors. Let's see now, what was we talking about? Oh, yes. You was telling me about your past life . . .

RED: My past life?

STAR: Yeah, there's a lot of things you about I'd like to know For instance what do they call you Red for? Your hair ain't no red.

RED: No, but they say my neck is.

STAR: Red neck? I know what that means. That means a Bolshevik!

RED: That's what they call any guy who's interested in saving somebody's skin beside his own. I try to get the workers decent living conditions, try to keep 'em from being exploited by the operators for all they're worth—and they call me a Bolshevik!

STAR: You know what's the matter with you? You take things too serious. You oughta come down off the soap-box oncet a while!

RED: I thought you was interested. You been coming to the meetings.

STAR: Yeah, I like to hear you talk, Red. It ain't what you say. It's just the sound of your voice. It kind of gets under my skin. [*Red is completely bemused. Star gets up and turns down the lamp very low, then sits down again.*] I don't like them fast hoe-downs. I like a sweet soundin' waltz, don't you?—Why don't you *SAY* somthin' you?!

RED [*drawling*]: I caint . . . .

STAR: Has the cat got your tongue?

RED [*slow drawl*]: When I look at you the way you are now I don't feel much like talkin'.

STAR [*rising*]: Maybe you'd rather dance, huh?

RED: Naw, I don't wanta dance neither.

STAR: Gosh, you're kind of hard to entertain!

RED: Naw, I'm not.

STAR: Maybe I just don't know how.

RED: It's easy . . . .

STAR: Gosh! You make me feel funny, just settin' there starin' at me like that. [*Crossing to table.*] I feel like I did the first time I ever had a date with a boy! Lissen—they're playin' a waltz tune now!

RED: Where did you get that honeysuckle from?

STAR: Down there in the hollow.

RED: Is there anymore down there?

STAR: It's plum full of it!

RED: I'd like a piece of it myself. To put under my pillow and dream on tonight. Come awn. Le's you an' me take a walk.

STAR: Where to?

RED: Down there in the hollow. By the spring. [*His voice lowers.*] There's a place down there where the water's real wide and smooth. You can see the stars in it as plain as you can in the sky!

STAR [*softly*]: I know. I go down there myself sometimes. That's where I was this evenin' when I got to feelin' so blue . . . .

RED: Maybe if you an' me went down together it wouldn't make you feel that way.

STAR: Maybe it would and maybe it wouldn't . . . .

RED: Take a chance on it, huh? [*Star smiles enigmatically.*] Star . . . .

STAR: Wait. I got a deck of cards here I tell fortunes with. [*She draws a much-worn deck from the table drawer.*] Pick a card!

RED [*grinning*]: Okay. [*He draws one and so does Star.*]

STAR: What you got?

RED: What did *you* get?

STAR: I'm callin' *YOU*!

RED: Well, I got the ace of spades!

STAR [*smiling*]: You're a liar, Birmin'ham Red! Lemme see?!

RED: Honest!

STAR: I know you didn't!

RED: Why? Did you have the deck stacked?

STAR: Lemme see that card?

RED [*grinning*]: Honest. It's the ace of spades! [*He tears it slowly in two, pushes back the lamp chimney and burns both halves. Then with his thumb he presses out the lamp wick. A square of moonlight comes through the window. The rest of the stage is intensely dark.*]

STAR [*softly, with a purring voice*]: You liar! You dirty *liar*!

RED: Star . . . .

STAR [*tenderly*]: You liar, you liar, you—*liar*!

[*The door is drawn slowly open, admitting a bar of moonlight; they go out; then it is drawn slowly closed. The music comes again more distinctly as though carried up by the wind. Then it fades almost into silence. After a moment Luke's voice is heard calling.*]

LUKE: Star—*Star!*

[*The door is pushed open. He calls her again. He sees she is gone. Then he goes on off down the road, still calling her name. The fiddles continue playing.*]

CURTAIN

SCENE FIVE

Scene: A few months later. Living room of Bram's cabin.

The stage is dark as the curtains rise except for faint streak of light from the kitchen where breakfast is being prepared, exactly as in the first scene of the play. The action at the beginning of this scene should follow closely as possible that of first scene, to suggest the sordid monotony of coal miners lives.

Bram, as in first scene, comes lumbering out of back room, stumbling against furniture and grumbling to himself. In his slow progress he upsets a chair.

FERN [*from kitchen*]: Good Lord, what a racket!

BRAM [*crossly*]: Wyncha turn the lamp on? Caint see a dern thing in here.

FERN: You oughta be used to the dark by now.

BRAM: Hester always had the lamp burnin' for me when I got up winter mornings. She known how bad my eyes was. She didn't want me falling and breaking my neck . . . . [*He lights the lamp. Pause.*]

FERN [*thrusting kettle through curtains*]: Here, Bram, go out an pump me a kettle full o' water.

BRAM [*grumbling*]: Hester had things ready. Didn't tell me to do this and that. You'd think I was— [*He goes out slamming the door—pause.*]

FERN [*coming in with bowls of porridge*]: Grumbles to himself like an old man. Getting kind of teched in the head, I suppose—Lord knows he didn't hurt himself doing things for her when she was living! Oh, *JOEL*!

JOEL[*off-stage*]: Coming!

FERN [*going back to door*]: Not so loud. You'll wake up Luke.

[*Bram has reentered.*]

FERN: Set down to your breakfast while it's hot.

BRAM [*sitting*]: Where's coffee.

FERN: Boiling.

BRAM: Can't you get things ready on time? Hester always did.

FERN: You know dern well she didn't. [*Going back to door and whispering tensely.*] Joel, come outa there and quit making all that noise.

[*There is a rap at front door. Fern opens the door to Tim Adams, the storekeeper. His manner is embarrassed.*]

TIM: Howdy, Mizz Pilcher.

FERN: Hello, Tim. Come in.

TIM: Mighty nasty weather we been havin' lately. [*Goes to right.*] Ole Hetty my sister's come down agin with the break-bone fever. Seems like every winter she has to come down with a spell.

FERN: That's bad. I guess you've come here for money agin?

TIM: Well, you know how it is, Mizz Pilcher. Gomstock's been kicking agin about givin' out so much credit. Fore God I got to collect on these here back bills or I'll git thrown out on my ear. That's orders. Nothing more from the store without cash and all the back bills paid up.

FERN: Bram! Tim wants money!

BRAM: Money? Who's got any money 'round here? All I got's scrip an' damn little of that. Here, take it all and God bless you! [*Fern takes it to Tim.*]

FERN: And he says we can't buy no more on credit.

TIM: That's right. It's on a straight cash basis now on. Company orders. [*Counting.*]

BRAM: Cash?

FERN: Think fast, Bram!

BRAM: Think fast about what?

FERN: You give him all the scrip you got and there ain't a scrap in the house for supper. [*She goes to the window.*]

TIM: Well, you know how it is, Mizz Pilcher. They useter run the company store for the mines but now they run the mines for the company store. The coal business is all shot to pieces. It's a wonder they don't quit operating altogether.

[*Joel enters.*]

JOEL: Hi, Tim. Gettin' any business since you fired me? [*He goes around below table to Tim.*]

TIM: Naw, even gittin' shut of you didn't do us much good. Well, I hope you all'll make out somehow. It ain't just you, you know, it's the whole camp—so long.

JOEL: So long, Tim.

[*Tim exits.*]

JOEL [*sitting in the middle chair*]: Kinda cold this morning, huh. Good possum weather! Where's coffee?

FERN: Coming. Set down and eat your mush.

[*She scurries outside to the kitchen for the coffee pot. Then returns. Luke appears in doorway. He is wearing the outfit of a miner. Fern goes to Joel's right. Luke looks sheepishly toward kitchen door. He and Joel exchange signs. Bram grunts vehemently and bends over food.*]

JOEL: Hey, Fern, pour *three* cups!

FERN [*from kitchen*]: *Three* cups? What for? I'm not drinkin' mine now. [*She hastens back in, at first not noticing Luke. Halfway to the table she see him, gasps, and stops short.*] *LUKE!* [*Her exclamation is in a tone of absolute terror.*]

BRAM [*jumping up*]: None of that foolishness, now! Luke's made up his mind. He's gonna go to work with me and Joel this morning.

JOEL [*grabbing coffee pot, which she had begun to empty on floor*]: Here, I'll take that! You're spilling what smells like pretty good coffee to me! [*He fills three cups on the table.*]

FERN [*in low stricken voice*]: Luke! [*She comes around the table.*]

LUKE: I'm sorry, Mother—I tried to tell you last night—I couldn't—I know how you feel about me going to work in the mines, but don't you see, it's . . . .

FERN [*facing Bram and Joel*]: You can't do this to me! [*She and Luke stand at the side door.*]

BRAM: Of all the doggone foolishness! Gimme that sugar—

JOEL: You'd think he was goin' out to rob a bank or something instead of doing an honest day's work in the mines, the way she's carrying on! Eat your breakfast, Luke and don't pay no attention to her.

[*Fern staggers against the wall.*]

LUKE: Mother! What's the matter?

FERN: Nothing. I'm all right. I just had such a funny feeling inside like something had fallen to pieces . . . Git those clothes off, Luke, and go back to bed. It ain't daybreak yet. You shouldn't try to scare me like that. It ain't right. I got too much to worry about as it is—Bram, there ain't no milk this morning. You'll have to drink your coffee black . . . .

BRAM: No milk, huh? Set down, Luke, and drink your coffee. We're gittin' late.

JOEL: Yeah, come on, Luke. Don't stand there gawking at her. She's just makin' a scene like they always do when they want to have their own way about something!

BRAM: No use you taking on like this, Fern. Luke's a grown boy now and he's goin' to work in the mines. Good Lord. I been through this with Hester so many times before that I'm good and sick of it I can tell ya! What's wrong with him being a coal miner? It's as honest, respectable work as a man can do!

FERN [*after a pause*]: What' wrong with it? It killed Luke's father, it did. It won't get Luke. I swore to myself, yes, I swore before God that I'd never let Luke go down in them mines. It ain't just for myself but for John, too, that I made up my mind against that. And it's over my dead body that he goes and that's no lie! You heard me, Luke. [*She moves toward him.*] Get back in there and take them mining things off. You ain't going down in the coal mines this morning or no time else! D'you hear me?

LUKE: Mother, won't you let me explain how it is? [*He is sitting now.*] It's not for good. Just for a few months. I need the money, Mom. We need two hundred more dollars than we got now if I'm gonna go through school in Tuscaloosa next fall . . . .

FERN: I'll raise it somehow. I earned most of it already and I can earn the rest. You see if I don't. But not this way, Luke. You'll never go down in them mines while I'm here to stop you. Now go back there and git them things off you and let's not have no more talk about—

JOEL [*getting up in exasperation*]: Leave him be, Fern. [*He goes around right of the table.*] You're crazy. There's nothing else for Luke to do. Is there, Luke? With things the way they are now, a man's good and lucky to get a job in the mines—'specially with them shut half the time and men laid off right and left. It was damned white of the "super" to say we could put Luke on. And we got a good spot for him, too, a new entry that's just been opened!

LUKE: Don't you see, Mother? [*He gets up.*]

FERN: I see, I see! I'll tell you what I see—I see your dead father's face when they took him up from the mines, when they carried him in to the house on a plank and pointed to it and said "That's your husband" and expected me to believe them. I can see those eyes of his staring at me like he was trying to think of something to tell me but couldn't . . . If he could've told me anything he would've told me to keep you out of the coal mines, Luke, and that's what I'm going to do!

BRAM [*getting up*]: Hester said the same thing about John and then about Joel. Both of them went on down in the mines— You caint stop 'em, Fern, the mines are in a man's blood . . .

[*Joel crosses back of rocker.*]

FERN: John hated the mines—I guess I should know. But it was the only thing he could do. [*Crosses to Joel.*] But Joel, you went to school. Hester saw to that. She even got you a job in the company store.

JOEL: I know she did. Mom was pretty swell. But it wasn't any use. Ole lady Abbey got me kicked out of the store. It wasn't my fault.

FERN: You didn't have to work in the mines. That's what killed Hester. That being underfed and overworked. But that was what finished her, when you went to work in the mines. She gave up and died then.

JOEL: What else could I do? Good Lord, I'm nearly twenty-two. Luke, he's seventeen. Both of us'll be wantin' homes of our own before long.

FERN: Luke's getting a real education. I'll see to that. I've been working my hands to the bone all these years . . . .

LUKE: That's what I don't want you to do any longer, Mom.

BRAM [*rising angrily*]: That's enough of all this here arguing back and forth. I'm the one that's running this house—if it hadn't been for me— [*He moves between Fern and Luke.*] —you and your boy would never set foot in that door. Hester was dead set against it—Joel, here, can bear me witness for that! Now come, Luke, drink your coffee and let's be goin'.

JOEL [*around back*]: Drink your coffee, Luke. You won't have nothing on your belly till supper if you don't. And believe me it's damn cold down there on that fifth level—

FERN [*breathlessly*]: The fifth level? [*She staggers to the rocker.*]

BRAM: Sure, the fifth level—what of it? [*Goes to stove.*]

FERN: No, no, not the fifth level. Luke, that's the one Star's man— [*She raises a hand to her mouth and gasps.*]

BRAM: Star's man WHAT?

FERN [*continuing with effort*]: That's the one Star's man said wasn't safe!

JOEL: Come on, Luke. She'll keep us here arguing all day if you let her! [*He takes Luke's arm and pulls him away from the table.*]

FERN [*screaming*]: Not the fifth level, Luke, not way down there! Star's man told her that the props down there ain't no good. They're like matchsticks, he said. They won't hold up. Oh, Luke, you can't go down there. Don't let him, Bram. Not down there, the fifth level, not down there—oh, please Luke!

LUKE [*going out door*]: Mother, it's no use. I've got to. It's—

JOEL: Come on. Quit arguing with her. [*He and Luke go out the door.*]

FERN [*desperately*]: He said it was too much weight, he knows. He said that they wouldn't hold up, they'll fall on you, Luke, you'll be killed down there! [*Bram moves toward her.*] Oh, my God, why don't you stop him, Bram. You can't let him go down there like that!

BRAM: I tell you, the boy's all right. That Bolshevik's a trouble-maker, he don't know a damned thing about mines— Now shut up and leave me be!—you've made us late already—

[*He crosses. Fern runs to the door and calls after them. Then she collapses moaning into the chair by the lamp.*]

FERN: I know, I know—I remember what happened to John. . . .

CURTAIN

SCENE SIX

Scene: The same.

It is about four-thirty in the afternoon of the same day, already getting dusk. Fern is preparing supper, slicing carrots and turnips into a large pot. She has an anxious, distracted air. Every few seconds she goes to the window, lifts the curtain, and peers out. After a while someone knocks. It is Star. Star is dressed and painted in her usual gay fashion but her manner is as anxious as Fern's.

FERN [*surprised*]: You—Star—

STAR: Yes, me. I know you don't want me here but I had to come. I get so lonesome sometimes I can't stand it no longer.

FERN: Come on in an' set down.

STAR: Thanks! [*Star seats herself in the rocking chair by the stove, and rocks tensely back and forth without speaking.*]

FERN: Look at your hands. They're cold as ice. What's happened?

[*Star says nothing.*]

FERN: Don't you want to tell me?

STAR: Yes, a-course I do. I can't keep it to myself no longer. It's—it's about—oh, Fern, why did I have to be such a damn fool! [*She jumps up from the chair and paces about the room.*]

FERN: Don't git yourself all wrought up like that. It won't help. Set down and I'll get you a cup of hot tea. [*As she goes offstage.*] What makes you think you're such a fool?

STAR: To get plumb gone on a man like this. It's too late for that now.

FERN: Red? [*She looks in.*] Set down, now, Star, and—

STAR: Oh, I can't set still. I've tried. I can't do it. Something in me wants to keep moving and won't let me stop. I've been just walking up and down like this for days and days while Red been down there in the mines. [*Fern comes back in to the table.*] Fern! You're good and quiet, that's why I felt like coming here to see you. I thought maybe—

FERN: Would you like a little rum in it?

STAR [*hysterically laughing*]: Rum? Oh, my God, yes. Hester always put rum in her tea. [*She sits.*]

FERN: I know she did. There ain't hardly none left now. I remember the first cup of rum tea I had in this house. It was the day I come here. A cold nasty day like this and Luke just a little boy then and me not knowing what to expect when I got here, how they'd treat me, what they'd say when I come—and soon as I got in the door, almost, Hester made me a cup of hot tea with a spot of rum in it—it was more than just a cup of tea, I remember—it was something like God's own mercy! That was more than ten years ago!

STAR [*sipping her tea*]: Yeah. It was the night after I left here. A lot of water's gone under the bridge since then— This tea's sure good.

FERN: Does it make you feel any better?

STAR: A whole lot.

FERN: It's about Red you've been worrying.

STAR: Yeah—him and the trouble at the mines.

FERN: Trouble! What trouble?

STAR: You ain't heard? They're talking strike.

FERN: Oh.

STAR: There ain't nothin' left to do. They's gotta be a showdown before long. God knows what'll happen then—

FERN: I don't hear much out of Bram and Joel—just a word here and there—now it's Luke—they've got Luke in the mines with them now!

STAR: Luke! Him in the mines!

FERN: Yes. They took him this morning.

STAR [*marveling*]: And you set here drinkin' tea! I thought you was determined they'd never catch Luke in the mines!

FERN: I was. So was Hester determined Bram wouldn't git Joel in the mines. Both of them are down there now. [*She stands up.*] On the fifth level!

STAR: The fifth level!

FERN: Yes, the one Red told you wasn't safe.

STAR [*indignantly*]: Red told me if he owned those mines he wouldn't send a yellow cur down there in that fifth level—the props are—

FERN: I know—you told me yesterday—like matchsticks! [*Pause. She covers her face with her hands and moves to inner doorway.*]

STAR: I guess I shouldn't have told you that. I was so worried about Red, him being down there—and this strike business! The men divided like they are against each other, half of them on Red's side, for the strike, and the others against him, scared of the company, and threatening him all the time—the damn fools! Red tries to make them see things but they won't! They'd rather go on as they are, the life being poisoned out of them with coal dust, overworked and underpaid, cheated, bought and sold—

FERN [*turning away*]: I didn't know you felt like that.

STAR: Oh, I didn't before. What did I care about the miners? Jake was my man and he worked in the mines a course. But I didn't love Jake. He brought me home money every week. Kept me. But I never cared about Jake very much. What kind of a life was that? It wasn't any at all. But with Red something's happened to me, Fern, I dunno what it is. I'm not like my old self anymore. It seems I've changed into somebody else and everything that I done before I look back at and wonder how it could have really been me that done those things—

FERN: I guess it wasn't you, really. You're in love with this man. [*Quietly.*] I know. I loved John like that.

STAR: And you lost him.

FERN: In the mines. [*Pause.*] And now Luke's gone. [*She goes to the window.*] It's getting dark. Turn the lamp on, Star.

STAR [*lighting the lamp*]: The same old lamp.

FERN: Yes. Hester's old lamp.

STAR: She used to sew by it nights.

FERN: I do too.

STAR: I can see her now setting there nights rocking back and forth with the look on her face never changing, just the shadows moving. I used to wonder what she was thinking about.

FERN: I know what she was thinking about.

STAR: Do you?

FERN: Yes, I'm a mother, too.

STAR: Oh! [*She lights another cigarette—near the stove.*] We all went back on her. None of us turned out like she wanted us to.

FERN: She wanted to keep her sons out of the mines. I know how that was. It was her life, all she lived for—the thing that kept her alive. After John's death it was Joel. She made me promise to save him from going the same way. But what could I do?

STAR: There was nothing for Joel but the mines.

FERN: And nothing for John.

STAR: And for me there was nothing but this.

FERN: You can thank God, Star, that you've got no sons.

STAR: Maybe things'll turn out diff'rent for Luke.

FERN: He's down there now. On the fifth level. That's where he is right this minute. [*She sits nervously in rocker.*] What time you'd guess it is, Star? It must be near closing time, ain't it?

STAR: Not long from it.

FERN: I got to think of some way to keep him from going back tomorrow. There must be some way.

STAR: Luke tole me you was saving money to send him to college.

FERN: Yes, but it ain't enough yet. I need a bit more. That's why Luke's down there working. He wants to go to Tuscaloosa next fall.

STAR: Well, it ain't for good, y'see. It's just til—

[*The whistle blows three times. The women sit erect, listening. Star rises stiffly, her eyes staring with terror. Fern cannot comprehend. She still sits in an erect, listening attitude, her head slightly on one side. The knife that she holds, paring vegetables, clatters to the floor. From outside there is a faintly audible rumble of running feet and shouting voices.*]

STAR: It blew—three times! [*She stands.*]

FERN: Star . . . .

STAR: *Three times*!

FERN: That means . . . .

STAR: Trouble at the mines!

FERN: *Star*!

STAR [*in a choked whisper*]: Trouble!

FERN: Yes. Trouble.

[*The clamor rises outside. Fern gets up stiffly from the chair. Her face is grotesque with fear, like a tragicomic mask. Star suddenly darts to the window.*]

FERN: *Star! Don't leave me! What d'you see?*

STAR: Everyone's running toward the shafts. Something's happened.

FERN: Something's happened. Star, don't leave me.

STAR: I couldn't go. My feet wouldn't carry me one step.

FERN [*incoherently mumbling*]: Don't go. Luke's down there. Something better for him than that. John went down there. What do you see now, Star? No, no, I can't look. Not now. Oh, my God, my dear God, don't let it be Luke this time.

STAR: They're coming this way, the whole crowd.

FERN: Don't let them see you standing there like that. They might see you, Star. They might come bringing him in on a plank! [*She sinks to her knees on the floor.*] Yes, I'm John's wife! What do you want with me now?

STAR [*joyously*]: It's not Red! I can see him. He's shouting and waving his arms! Thank God!!

FERN: John's wife. Yes, that's me. You ought to know me by now. I've been here long enough God knows! [*She laughs hysterically and covers her face with her hands.*]

STAR: I can see Bram, too. He's coming first, in front of the men. Oh, Fern— [*Her voice lowers with anxiety.*] They're coming this way! [*She back away from the window.*]

FERN: No, No! [*Gets up. Her voice raises to a scream.*] No, no! They can't come here! John's dead! A long time ago! Not now! It couldn't happen again! For God's sake come away from the window! [*She pulls desperately at Star's arm.*] Don't let them see you standing there. They'll bring him in dead on a plank and—

[*From outside comes Red's voice to mob.*]

RED: I told the bloody bastards that it wasn't safe. They laughed in my face. You'll work down there or you'll get the hell out, they said. I told the foreman yesterday that the props were no good, that they wouldn't hold up—he said if I wanted new ones I could cut them myself! [*He turns to the men.*] What're you going to do about it? Nothing? Or will you show those murderers that you're men now—and *fight*!

[*A loud roar of fury rises from the men outside the cabin. Torches flare through the windows. The clamor and shouting rises louder. Star and Fern both retreat slowly from the window to inner door. The door is thrown open. Bram stands there, panting, his eyes staring blindly.*]

BRAM: Where's Fern? I can't see.

STAR [*taking a few steps*]: She's here. [*She points to Fern who has sunk to the floor.*]

BRAM: You—Star.

STAR: Yes.

BRAM [*after a long pause*]: Tell Fern it's not her boy.

STAR: Fern! Do you hear? Bram says it's not Luke!

[*Men enter carrying a body laid out on a plank, the head covered. Other men crowd behind, but everyone is now silent, staring at Bram and Fern. Bram crosses to Fern.*]

BRAM [*dully*]: Does she hear? It's not Luke. Tell her again.

STAR [*seizing Fern's shoulder*]: Fern! Fern!

FERN [*moaning*]: Luke!

STAR: Listen, Fern, it's not Luke. Bram says to tell you it's not Luke!

FERN [*wildly*]: Not Luke? You're lying! John's dead. It's got to be Luke this time! [*She sees the body on the plank and screams.*]

BRAM [*stepping forward and clutching her arm*]: It's not your boy.

FERN: It's Hester's boy. It's Joel.

[*Bram goes off. Luke breaks through the doorway. Fern and Luke are at the extreme right. Red and the men are with the body stage center.*]

CURTAIN

SCENE SEVEN — THE WAKE

Scene: Bram's cabin. That evening.

The body is laid out in the back room where the women mourners congregate. The men are seated in the front room around the stove. As the curtains open we see Bram, Luke, an aged religious zealot named Whitey Sunter and a hard-drinking Irishman, Sean O'Connor. Bram's face is stony with the hard repressed grief of his kind. He stares fixedly at the stove or wall. The table is against the wall, Luke is to the extreme left, Whitey is just left of center, Sean nearer Luke.

WHITEY: There's been a pow'ful lot o' divilment round this here camp. Sech goins-on as I never known in my time. Infi-duls and Jeze-buls! Carryin' on in a scand'lous way. Livin' togither unwedded. [*He casts a significant eye at Bram.*] It's a fault on Christian upbringin'. If these here infiduls an Jezebuls had been brought up Christian-like as I brung up my childern they never would come to no sech a state o' sinfulness.

SEAN [*taking a swig*]: It's the niggers an' furriners raise the divil round here.

WHITEY: It's a visitation o' the Lord, that's what it is! He's lit the divil loose in Clay County.

SEAN: Red Hill country's the divil's own stampin' groun ever since creation if y'ask my 'pinion.

[*He belches loudly and offers the bottle to Whitey, who abjures it with a gesture of righteous disdain. Sean takes another long drag and carefully places the bottle under his chair. There is a knock. Luke goes to the door. A number of women enter, admitted by Luke. They are led by Ethel Sunter.*]

ETHEL [*in a high-pitched, whining voice*]: Bless the Lord, brothers. The Lord giveth and the Lord taketh away!

WHITEY: A-men!

ETHEL [*in a professional tone*]: Where's the body laid out?

BRAM [*without looking up*]: Back room.

ETHEL [*efficiently marshaling her flock*]: Come on, sisters. You too, Pappy. We'll start off the prayer readin' naow. [*She sniffs the air.*] *Likker*! [*Sean returns her baleful glare without shame.*] Somebody I could mention's got no more sense o' decency and shame than a—than a . . . .

SEAN: Than a what?

ETHEL: Hmph! Come, Pappy!

SEAN [*in a low but distinct drawl*]: Somebody I could mention's got a nose that ud make a pretty good fishin' pole.

BRAM [*with suppressed fury*]: Shut up!

ETHEL [*turning at the door*]: Those that ain't been saved ud better not come in while prayer's bein' offered.

WHITEY: Those that ain't been praperly baptized is infiduls in the eyes o' the Lord.

SEAN: Who's an infidul you ole billy goat?

BRAM [*warningly*]: Shut up, you!

[*The door is closed on the back room. After a moment we hear Whitey intoning a long exhortation. Luke gets up and moves nervously about the cabin.*]

LUKE: Why do they have to make all that fuss? There's something not decent about it!

SEAN [*raising bottle*]: The ole billy goat an' his nanny!

BRAM: Shut up!

LUKE: Why don't they dig him a grave put him down in it and be done? That's the way Joel would've wanted it done. He wouldn't have wanted all that cheap hypocritical slobbering over his . . . .

BRAM [*more sharply*]: Shut up!

LUKE: He'd have wanted a clean quick burying out in the woods without any fuss to it, that's what Joel would've wanted. He'd've wanted you to lay him away right now in the dark out there on the hills where he used to hunt possum at night with his dog.

SEAN [*casually*]: Good possum-hunting weather now. Wish I had me a good possum dog. The persimmons're gittin' ripe. Bet I could tree me a possum in less'n five minutes with a good possum-hunting dog!

[*Bram bows his head lower.*]

LUKE: Joel liked the woods. He used to spend pretty near all his time in the woods when he wasn't workin.

SEAN: Joel was a good squirrel shot. I seen him drap one on the top branch o' that ole oak on Bald Ridge standin' off at a distance of about fifty-sixty yards. Drapped him dead at one shot. Joel was a dead-eye with a rifle. But never could handle a shotgun. I remember first time he ever fired a shotgun he was a little tike about ten or 'leven an' the kick of it knocked him flat on his back. I guess he never got the proper feel of one since.

LUKE: It's the woods he ought be laid in, not any ole weedy graveyard.

SEAN: Joel had a pretty good rifle. Guess you'll be usin' it now, won't you, Luke? Wish I had me a good rifle an' a good huntin' dawg!

LUKE: He oughta be buried out in the woods where he buried his dog. Up there in the hills where they used to go huntin' possum togither. That ole possum dog was Joe's best friend. When he died las' summer Joel buried him under a persimmon tree out there in the hills 'cause he said when fall come and the possums crawl out on the limbs to eat persimmons at night, he bet ole Spot's ghost ud rise up from his grave an' start up such an awful leapin' an bayin' that the possum's ud git so scared they'd shake the persimmons all off the tree.

SEAN [*after a pause*]: What would you all take for Joel's ole rifle?

LUKE: That's where Joel oughta be buried. Out there on the hills under that ole persimmon tree.

BRAM [*rising in anguish*]: Quit talking! Quit talking! [*He regains his stern composure.*] Joel's body gits buried in a decent Baptist cimitary like all his folks was before him! [*He crosses to the inner door and looks off, then he sits in the far corner.*]

SEAN [*taking a drink*]: I reckon Joel don't care much where they lay him now. One place's good as another. Maybe he's kinda lucky that he cleared out before all this strike business gits started. No tellin' what's gonna come of it all. Well, strike or no strike things caint git no worse than they already are. [*He yawns and rests his feet on the stove top.*]

BRAM: Strike?

SEAN: Yeah.

BRAM [*showing dull interest*]: What strike?

SEAN: Ain't you heard about the men goin' out on strike tomorrer?

BRAM: No.

SEAN: It was your boy gittin' kilt that made 'em decide so sudden on doin' it. They figger that Joel was as good as murdered. That's what Birmin'ham Red called it. Cold-blooded murder. He said he told ole Abbey them props wouldn't hold an' Abbey told him if he wanted more he could go an cut 'em himself!

LUKE: The God-damn—

BRAM: Shut up on that kind of talk! What good's strike gonna do 'em?

SEAN: Should think you'd be in favor of it seein' as how it was your own boy.

BRAM: What good would making trouble do me? It wouldn't bring Joel back alive.

LUKE: There's others beside Joel.

BRAM: I started to work in them mines when I was ten years old and I been workin' in 'em ever since.

SEAN: So've I.

BRAM: Year in, year out, and I'll go on workin' in 'em til the day that I die, so help me. That's my job. [*He moves his chair closer to the stove.*] My oldest boy John got killed in the mines, too. He was kilt up North in the anthracite fields. Run down by an enjin in one o' the entries. Seems like they made the entry too narrow long there for a man and a car to pass the same time an' he got smashed up against the rib and tore all to pieces.

SEAN: God!

BRAM: But if you think I'm gonna uphold this here strike cause I lost my two boys in the mines, you're wrong, dead wrong.

SEAN: Well, whether you want it or not, the men's gonna strike. Birmin'ham Red's got 'em all worked up to a fever. That's why none of 'em have shown up here. They're over at that mass-meetin' he's holdin'. There won't be no coal dug out tomorrer.

BRAM: I'll be diggin' mine out.

SEAN: Then they'd call you a scab.

BRAM: Let 'em call me a scab. Let 'em call me any damn thing they want.

SEAN: You caint tell what men'll do when they git wrought up.

BRAM: Let 'em do what they want. I ain't going out on no strike.

SEAN: You know how things've been.

BRAM: Sure I know how things've been.

SEAN: There's starvation, plain starvation, here in this camp.

BRAM: An' there'll be a lot more if they start up a strike. Who's gonna feed 'em? They ain't got food enough with the store closed up to last 'em three days.

SEAN: I reckon they'll be goin' hungry tomorrer if the store's shut down.

BRAM: What's to keep it frum shuttin' if they strike?

LUKE: Nothin'. It'll shut down right away.

BRAM: What do they think they'll live on?

LUKE: Maybe have some food shipped in.

SEAN: Yeah.

BRAM: How'll they pay for it?

SEAN: Take up a collection, I reckon.

BRAM: Collect what? Scrip?

SEAN: That's right. I never had thought o' that. Huh. Luke.

LUKE: I reckon Mom's the only person in camp's got any real money.

SEAN [*alertly*]: She's got money? [*He looks to Luke.*]

BRAM: Saved up for sendin' Luke off to college.

SEAN: Maybe she'd loan it.

BRAM: Loan it? On what?

SEAN: Hmmm. Reckon it'd be takin' a risk all right.

LUKE: If it was mine I'd give it.

BRAM: It ain't yours an' you'll keep your hands off it.

[*A group of miners enter, about ten or fifteen. Silently filing with bowed heads into the back room and then out, taking places along the wall. Some women go inside—Bram stands near the inner door with a group.*]

SEAN: You boys come from the meetin'?

FIRST MINER: Yeah.

SEAN: What's up?

FIRST MINER: Strike!

SEAN: Strike?

CHORUS OF MINERS: Strike!

SEAN: That's the stuff! It shoulda come before this.

[*There is an excited murmur among the men. Sean is showing off. He rises and makes emphatic gestures, passing along the wall, talking to the men. Bram remains stolidly indifferent. Luke looks on with intense interest.*]

SEAN: We gotta live, ain't we? Sure we gotta live!

CHORUS OF MINERS: We gotta live!

SECOND MINER: Ain't got no right to starve us.

SEAN: Bury us alive! [*An angry murmur rises from the miners.*]

BRAM [*rising*]: How'll you live if you quit work and the store shuts down?

FIRST MINER: We couldn't be no worse off than we are already. They don't even pay us no more. Give us pieces of paper. Scrip. Twelve-and-a-half cents a ton. Do you call that pay?

CHORUS OF MINERS: Hell, no!

SECOND MINER: Monday I worked sixteen hours down there on the fifth level where they had the cave-in today. Loaded up twelve cars, fifteen ton each. Tipple crew weighed me for less than eighty tons when I checked out.

FIRST MINER: They paid me a dollar in scrip. Outa that I had to buy carbine an' powder for my next day's work. I had to pay for a bit that got broke through no fault of my own. I had ten cents left for supper—a dime to eat on.

SECOND MINER: You're lucky you ain't got a wife an' six kids.

[*An angry murmur comes from the Chorus.*]

THIRD MINER: My kids're swole up in the belly frum not gittin' fed.

SECOND MINER: Yestiddy I caught my youngest puttin' dirt in her mouth.

THIRD MINER: Hell, mine eat grass for supper!

FIRST MINER: We're human, ain't we?

SECOND MINER: No, the operators're human but we ain't.

THIRD MINER: By God I know my ole woman's human.

FIRST MINER: We're all human.

SECOND MINER: What do you say, Bram? Are you with us?

BRAM: I ain't with no strikers if that's what you mean. Strikin' won't do you no good. Blind as I am I can see a damn sight more plain than you can about that.

TIM ADAMS: It ain't the company's fault. There's a depression in the coal industry, like everything else. They got to cut their prices to meet competition.

FIRST MINER: Okay, cut prices. But who pays for it?

CHORUS OF MINERS: We do!

FIRST MINER: Do they dig down in their own bank vaults?

SECOND MINER: Hell, no they take it out of our lunch boxes!

TIM: Why, it ain't even profitable to keep these mines runnin' at the present price o' coal. If it wasn't for the company store they'd have to shut down.

FIRST MINER: They shut down up in Pennsylvainy for eighteen months. Miners took to bootleggin'. Diggin' out coal themselves and sellin' it. Operators caint do nothin' about it.

TIM: That ain't legal.

THIRD MINER: What of it?

FIRST MINER: We got to live somehow!

CHORUS OF MINERS: We gotta live!

SEAN [*wanting to hold the show*]: We don't want talk. We want ACTION! We been askin' it long enough around here. Now we start dishin' it out. These sonsabitches, whadathey think they are, huh? I guess we got our constitutional rights. Wahddayasay? Vote the straight Democratic ticket in every election they ever had in this goddam state of Alabama. Yezzir. Run out the niggers, keep the lousy furriners out, we'll have a free country someday, these goddamn sonsabitches caint keep us down on our bellies in dirt, we got our constitutional rights, they respeck em or by God we'll have the biggest necktie party state of Alabama, I'll tell the cockeyed world!

[*Bram rises and pushes him violently in the face. Sean falls to the floor.*]

BRAM: Shut up. Shut yer blasted mouth.

[*There are murmurs from the miners.*]

BRAM: Shut up all of you.

FERN [*entering*]: Bram. [*Silence.*] Your last son's layin' dead in there. Ain't you got no decent feelings for the dead?

[*Song and prayer are heard from other room.*]

LUKE: Why can't they leave him be? Joel don't want that. He wants a clean quick buryin'. He doesn't want to be slobbered over by a bunch of groaning old women. Can't they let him alone in there?

BRAM: Stop!

[*As the song rises — Fern puts her hand over Luke's mouth.*]

CURTAIN

SCENE EIGHT

Scene: Star's cabin. One or two nights later.

The curtains open on a lamp-lit interior. Red sits by the stove. Star wears a loud black-and-white checked skirt with a red blouse and gold bracelets that jangle on her wrists like manacles. Star paces about the room, looking now and then through the burlap-curtained window. Red is at the table playing solitaire.

RED: Caint you quit walking up and down like that? It gives me the jitters.

STAR: Well, at least make a little noise. [*She is near him.*] It's so quiet now you can hear the ice dropping off the roof. [*She turns to the window.*] You can almost hear yourself think. What's going to happen around this place anyhow?

RED [*sitting down at table and writing*]: I wish I could tell you.

STAR: I never known it so quiet in my life. It makes me feel like something awful was hanging over my head, getting ready to fall the next minute. [*She pulls a jug from under the bed and is pouring drinks during the following lines.*] I thought strikes made more noise than this. [*To window.*] I thought people shouted and threw things and made a big crash-boom-bang! [*She laughs nervously.*] Now everybody's inside with the windows covered up like they was hiding from something. Store's closed. Everything's closed up. Even people's mouths. They don't even say nothing to each other.

RED [*bitterly*]: No. They're scared to. They need something to put the fight back in them.

STAR: What most of 'em need's a square meal. When's that glorious relief gonna come to the rescue?

RED: Soon as they can.

STAR: Soon as they can? That might be next Christmas. Or maybe April Fool's Day.

RED: I figure a week or ten days.

STAR: That ain't soon enough.

RED: I know it.

STAR: If they don't git food right away they're bound to give up. Sure ain't a scrap to eat in camp—and the store's closed. Gomstock pulled a pretty smart trick when he had all the stock trucked outa the store before he shut it down. Now there ain't even a thing left to steal. How long d'you think they'll be holdin' out on empty stomachs?

RED: We got a truck. We could get supplies from Oakland if we had the money.

STAR: There's been nothing but scrip in camp for months and not much of that.

RED: There's three hundred dollars in camp.

STAR: You're crazy! Where is it? [*She moves toward him.*]

RED: Luke's mother.

STAR: Fern? Oh! You won't get that.

RED: Why not?

STAR: You think she'd give that up?

RED: I'm counting on it.

STAR: She worked ten years for it. Doing washing. So's she could send Luke to school in Tuscaloosa. She'd sooner quit breathing.

RED: It's the only money in camp. We've got to have it. The strike depends on it.

STAR: The strike could go to blazes before she'd part with any of Luke's college money! [*She picks up the cups.*]

RED: How do you know?

STAR: I'm a woman and she's one, too. Our own men's all we care about.

RED: Maybe some women ain't as selfish as you give 'em credit for.

STAR: That's just one of your boy scout ideas. [*She goes for the whiskey.*] Fern won't give up her money. You're barking up the wrong tree, old boy.

RED: If she don't we're washed up. With that money we could feed the camp for two weeks. She wouldn't hold out on the whole camp that way.

STAR: Huh! That's what you think! I guess you need a drink. [*She replaces the jug under the bed.*]

RED: What makes that jangling noise every time you move?

STAR: My bracelets. Why?

RED: Take the damn things off. They sound like chains rattling.

STAR: God knows we need something to make some noise around here. [*She hands him a tin cup of whiskey.*] Toss it down. There's nothing like a shot of corn to cure the jitters.

RED: Where did you get that rot-gut from?

STAR: Never mind where I got it. Just drink up and see if it ain't what the doctor ordered. Forget about this strike business. People got to go on living strike or no strike . . . .

RED: I don't want whiskey. What kind of a dog do you think I am? There's kids in camp that havin't got milk to drink and I'm not gonna lap up whiskey so I can forget it!

STAR: Oh, act human for a change. Don't you ever git tired of acting like a saint around here? [*She drinks and as she moves the bracelets jangle.*]

RED: Take those jangling things off!

STAR: I won't.

[*Red seizes her and tears off the bracelets.*]

STAR: My fav'rite bracelet. [*She automatically stoops to pick up fragments.*]

RED: Star, why don't you— [*He turns.*]

STAR: Why don't I what? Go on and say it!

RED: Maybe I'd better move out of here.

STAR [*slowly*]: No, you can't do that. [*She comes to him.*]

RED: It ain't safe for you.

STAR: How do you mean not safe?

RED: Me being here.

STAR: You mean there might be trouble?

RED: There's bound to be. [*He goes to the window.*]

STAR: What's safe for you's safe for me!

RED: Anything might happen. Tonight or tomorrow.

STAR [*after a pause*]: Ain't you got sense enough to see I'm plumb gone on you?

RED: I ain't got time for that. [*He turns slightly.*]

STAR: When will you have time?

RED: This thing's first. That's got to wait.

STAR: You'll never have time if you stay around here!

RED: Maybe not.

STAR: You don't know how sweet life could be for you or you couldn't wait so easy. I wanted a lot of things I've never got. I know how swell it would be to get things you wanted always. I want things, Red, that you and I could give each other. A real home and kids. [*She goes to the lower end of bed.*]

RED: That's new ain't it? I thought you didn't want no part of that.

STAR: I didn't. Not with no other man but you. You're the first.

RED: Yeah? You wanted freedom. You didn't want to be tied down you said.

STAR: I didn't want to be tied down with Jake Walland or any of his kind. That's what I meant by wanting freedom. Now I don't want it anymore. I want the kind of life that you could give me and if I can't have that kind of life, Red? I don't want any kind of life at all. Yeah. That's how gone I am!

RED [*rolling a cigarette*]: All I can say is you're making an awful fool of yourself. [*He walks to the table.*]

STAR: You don't mean that.

RED: I do. I'm not a woman's man.

STAR: What kind of a man are you? I can't figure it out. Sometimes I look at you and I feel like I was looking at somebody I never seen before in my life. There's two of you I guess.

RED: Two of me?

STAR: Yeah, one of you's a flesh and blood man. The other's someone else and he *hates* me.

RED: You're wrong about that. He don't hate you. Star, he's just afraid of you because he's got a big job to do and he's afraid that you might try to stop him. [*Luke knocks—Star stands up.*]

RED: Who's that?

LUKE [*in a low tone*]: Me.

RED: Oh, it's Luke. [*Red lets him in.*] What's up?

LUKE [*a little breathlessly*]: I thought I better tell you — a truck-load of men just come into camp.

RED: Yeah?

LUKE: They're holding some kind of confab down in the basement of the company store.

RED: What'd they look like? [*He grabs Luke.*]

LUKE: I didn't get a look at them. They drove up without any headlights and stashed the truck out in the woods back of the store. Some of us snuck back there to look at it and—

STAR: Red, it's the—

LUKE: So what? Maybe it's a good thing they decided to start something. Joel Pilcher's getting smashed wasn't enough. What we're spoiling for's a good fight! [*He goes to the window.*]

LUKE: You better round the men up.

RED: No. Let the Rover boys make the first move.

STAR: Red! You're the one they'll come for first. The lamp! [*She suddenly turns the lamp out.*]

RED [*angrily*]: What did you blow that out for?

STAR: They could shoot you through the window, you fool!

RED: Well, that's my funeral. Turn the lamp back on. [*Luke relights the lamp with a dim flame so that most of the room is in shadow.*]

STAR: Red, you can't stay here! [*She comes to him at the window.*] You've got to hide somewhere.

RED: Me hide? [*He goes to table and turns to Luke.*] Did you get it? [*There is silence.*] The money! Did you get it?

LUKE [*in a strained whisper*]: Yes. [*Reaches into pocket and pulls out a roll of bills.*]

RED [*eagerly taking the money*]: What luck! This'll see us th[r]ough a couple of weeks! Luke, your mother's won this fight for us! You tell her that for me, Luke! It will be her sacrifice that done it!

LUKE: I can't tell her. [*He moves to the inner door.*]

STAR: Red, you give him back that money! You fool, don't you see he's stole it from her! [*She runs to Red.*]

RED: Stole it! No! She gave it to him! Luke?

LUKE [*turns*]: Yeah. I stole it from her. I had to. You see—she wouldn't give it up. I seen it wasn't any use asking her so I waited til she'd gone out and found where she kept it hid—under a loose board—an' I stole it!

STAR: Give it back to him, Red. He ain't got a right to steal from his mother like that.

RED: You asked her for it and she wouldn't—?

LUKE: She wouldn't hear of it. She nearly went crazy when I asked her.

RED: And so you stole it from her?

LUKE: I had to. We got to buy food for the camp.

STAR: You ain't keeping it are you, Red?

RED [*after a pause*]: Sure I'm keeping it! [*He turns to Star.*]

STAR: You'll make a thief of Luke?

RED: *I'm* the one who stole this money.

STAR: Yeah, and Fern'll have you locked up for it mor'n likely!

RED: We'll drive over to Oakland and buy a truckload of rations in the morning. Luke, you better take Star home with you.

STAR: Take me? This here's my cabin. I'm not going nowhere. [*She goes to the window.*]

RED: Stay away from that window. Go on home, Luke.

LUKE: I'm staying, too.

RED: I'm not asking you to go, I'm telling you. Go on!

LUKE: I can't face her now.

STAR [*at the window*]: You've got to. She's coming here right now.

LUKE: I can't face her! [*He moves away from the door.*]

STAR [*opening the door*]: He's here.

FERN [*entering*]: Luke! I thought this was where I'd find you. [*She turns to Red.*]

[*Luke turns his back on Fern. Red and Fern face each other.*]

FERN [*furiously*]: You, Red, what've you done with it! [*Red looks at her without speaking.*] My money! I know you got it. You was after it. Luke told me so. Now give it right back to me!

STAR [*at the window*]: Give it back to her, Red.

FERN: Give it right back to me this minute!

RED: I guess I had the wrong slant. Star was right. I was barking up the wrong tree . . . .

FERN: You give it back to me!

LUKE [*starting to protest—turning*]: Mom, I—

FERN: You, Luke! How could you steal from me like that?

RED: I told him to ask you for it—you wouldn't let him have it.

FERN: Let him have it! Why should I? I worked for that money ten years!

RED: You know what it's needed for?

FERN: Yes, I know what *you* want it for. I want it for Luke. It's Luke's money, all of it, saved up for him!

LUKE: I won't take it! [*He walks to the table.*]

FERN: Oh, it ain't just for you neither. It was for your father too. It was to pay him back something I owed him. He never got a chance to live decent like he wanted to. I was going to see that you did. And a woman don't work ten years like a dog for nothin'!

RED: Nothing?

FERN [*her voice hoarse with bitterness*]: John was buried in a pauper's grave. In a plain box coffin with the lid nailed down. There's a dumpyard off at the side that stinks of garbage. The day they buried him the wind was blowing from that direction and instead of crying over his grave, I got sick at the stomach. That was our last goodbye. And that was a sweet one, wasn't it? I didn't have money enough to buy him a stone to put over his head. When I come down here I thought maybe I could earn him one. So I took in washing. But after a while it struck me that maybe I could put up something better than a tombstone for him to be remembered by. Luke was so much like him. He was John all over again. A life that come out of him. But I could make Luke everything that John couldn't be. And that would suit him a whole lot better I thought than a stone with his name and a couple of dates carved on it! That's what I been working for ten years and I ain't going to give it all up for nothing! [*She sinks onto the stool—Star sits near her.*]

RED [*waiting til she has calmed somewhat before speaking*]: For nothing? There's fifteen hundred people in camp. Do you call them nothing? [*He goes to her.*]

FERN: Only one of them's my son!

RED: Why not the others?

FERN: The others?

RED [*still quietly*]: John was a coal miner, wasn't he?

FERN: He was *killed* in the mines! But not Luke—he's gonna get away.

RED [*looking at Luke*]: Away where? To Heaven and play on harps?

FERN: Someplace. Away of all this!

RED [*sarcastically*]: Oh, Beulah land, my Beulah land! Beautiful isle of somewhere! The land of brotherly love—the land at the end of the rainbow where you find the big pot of gold—the land of the lemonade rivers and the sugar cake trees—the land where they shingle their houses with gooseberry pies! Yeah, I've heard about it in fairy stories. That's where you want Luke to go. I've always had a hankerin' for a place like that myself. A place where they don't have locks and fences 'cause every man loves his neighbor . . . a nice place, huh? When you get there, Luke, I wish you'd pick me out a corner lot in the suburbs. Not too far off the car-line. You know, a place with southern exposure and a good view of the sunset . . . . [*He bursts into derisive laughter.*]

STAR: Quit kiddin' her, Red. This ain't no jokin' matter.

RED: Excuse me, lady. I'm in a fanciful humor tonight. I guess that comes of not over-eating . [*He lights a cigarette, walks to table, then to window, and then comes to Fern and speaks harshly.*] There ain't no place like that. I'm a guy that knows. It's all over this world you got to fight and fight hard to go on living and you can't get out of it by moving to no other place this side of Jordan!

FERN: There must be peace somewhere!

RED: If there is, lady, I must've overlooked it. Peace is something a guy's got to make for himself. It ain't a thing he happens to come across like a four-leaf clover. Or a nickel somebody lost in an alley. It's something he's got to work for himself. And he's usually got to fight for it, too. Running away don't help. What good would that do?

FERN: I owe it to John to see that Luke gets his chance!

RED: D'you think John would want his boy to lam out of a fight all his own people was in?

FERN: I don't know . . . .

RED: Yes, you do. You remember him too well not to. It's plain as daylight. I know John thru and thru cause I know his boy—Luke his livin' breathin' image—John's monument. Do you think he'd be proud of the choices you've made? He wasn't the first to die in the mines. There was lots of others. Death after death. And some of them not so quick. They could write starvation on pretty near every death ticket they filled out around here and it wouldn't be very far off. And now these people are fighting for a chance to live. Isn't that a big enough monument for John—to give 1500 of his own people their last fightin' chance on earth? There's your money on the table . . . take it or leave it . . . you have your choice . . . .

FERN [*crossing to him*]: You talk so fast I can't think . . . .

RED: You don't need to think. Let your man think for you. Ask John what to do with the money.

FERN: John?

RED: Yeah . . . let him tell you what to do with it . . . .

FERN: John . . . [*She turns with a bewildered gesture to Luke.*]

LUKE: Let the men have the money, Mom.

FERN: Yes, John. They can have the money. Luke will have to get along without it somehow . . . . [*She turns to her left toward the door, her movements halting and stiff. She goes out.*]

STAR [*with a pitying gesture*]: Fern . . . .

RED [*to Luke*]: Go with your mother, boy.

MUSIC — CURTAIN

SCENE NINE

Scene: The same.

STAR: Red, what're you going to do now?

RED: Nothing.

STAR: Are ya just gonna stay here and wait for them to come and get you?

RED: Somebody's got to get it in the neck. I guess I'm the logical candidate. [*Pause.*]

STAR: What are you doing this for?

RED: *What* am I doing?

STAR: You're throwing yourself away. Those men've come here to *kill* you. You oughta know that. [*Pause.*]

RED: What did Luke's mother give me the money for?

STAR: I dunno. Fern must've lost her senses!

RED: No, she didn't. She saw something all of a sudden that she never had seen before!

STAR [*sarcastically*]: Oh, she saw the light, huh? [*Pause.*]

RED: Yeah. That's a pretty good way of putting it.

STAR: She looked to me like she was struck blind.

RED: Maybe she was for a minute. There's a lot of difference between looking at a candle and then looking at the sun.

STAR: You say a lot of things that don't make sense, Red. If I got down on my knees and begged you to, would you do it?

RED: What?

STAR: Get me out of this!

RED: Sure, you can go. I told you to go on home with Luke and Fern.

STAR: You don't love me. You don't give a damn for me!

RED: You know I do, Star. [*He speaks with momentary tenderness.*] You're the only woman that ever rated a dime's worth with me. But loving and fighting are two different things. You can't mix 'em.

STAR: Isn't there a way out for us, Red?

RED: Maybe next spring we'll go north with all of this left behind us. Then there'll be plenty of time to talk about love. Those things you said that you wanted. I'm human too. Maybe you doubt that sometimes because I seem hard. I'm not hard. [*His voice deepens.*] When I look at you I go soft inside, so soft that it scares me. I want to put my hands on you and never take them off!

STAR [*approaching him*]: Why don't you? I like your hands! When you were talking at the meetins I used to look at your hands and feel them touchin' me! Sometimes I could even feel them striking me and I liked even that! I wanted to get in front of your hands and feel them poundin' me down, down! I knew from the very beginning that it would be like that! Your hands beating me down! And still I wanted it, Red. I wanted to feel your hands on my body! Knockin' me down or squeezin' me tight against you like this!

[*They embrace passionately for a minute.*]

RED: Star.

STAR: What?

RED: You're like fire in my blood!

STAR [*eagerly*]: You'll go? [*They embrace again. Pause.*] You'll go—you'll go—

RED [*steeling himself*]: Not now! I can't, I can't! Next spring. [*He breaks away.*]

STAR: Spring's a long way off!

RED: Not so long. You can hear the ice dripping off the roof now.

STAR: Lots of things can happen between now and spring.

RED: I've got to take a chance on that.

STAR: It's too big a chance! Red, do you know what's going to happen? I can feel it comin' just as sure as I could feel your hands on me the first time I saw you walkin' down that street out there! You've got to go away with me, Red! [*She is talking to his back.*]

RED: When I go away it'll be because I won, not because I got beat.

STAR: Maybe you won't win or lose. Maybe you'll just be—[*She gasps.*]

RED: Pushing up daisies? [*He crosses to the cot and lies down.*] It's no use, Star. We got to wait til this thing's over.

STAR [*going and kneeling on floor near head of bed*]: But I can't wait—I want you now Red. All of you. Not just part. Maybe I'm sort of blind in one eye or something but I can't see things your way. All I can see, all I can think of, is just *us*, you and me, the rest don't matter!

RED: That's not being blind, I guess. That's just being a woman. [*He lies down on the cot. She seats herself beside him.*] I could feel the same way.

STAR: Could you, Red?

RED [*lighting a cigarette*]: Sure I could, If I'd let myself.

STAR [*also lighting a cigarette*]: Well, why don't you then? Why don't you stop trying to be a tin god? What do you get out of it, anyway?

RED: Something bigger than me.

STAR: What's that?

RED: You wouldn't know.

STAR: No, I guess I wouldn't!

RED: I didn't either for a long time. I had to leave the best part of my life behind me before I began to understand what I was living for. I used to live like you. Just for myself and my own good. Or maybe some dame that had me bothered. I thought that was all that mattered. Then up north in the anthracite fields, the workers were starving. My brother was working along trying to help and I saw him get struck down with a brick bat by a bunch of thugs that the operators had hired to dust him off. They cracked his head open. Killed him. Just for trying to help his own people over a tough spot. I guess that changed me. Ever since I've wanted to fight, not for myself, not for my own gain, but for all the other poor lunks that don't get a square deal . . . [*He sits up on cot.*] Ain't that something worth fighting for?

STAR [*stands up*]: All I know is I love you and I want you for myself. The rest I can't see. Oh, Red, I don't want nothing to happen to you! [*She throws herself down on the cot besides him. She grabs him.*] If anything happened. I couldn't stand it, Red! [*Sobbing.*] Something inside of me just aches when you ain't with me. Just to think. If that was to go on all the time I couldn't stand it, Red. I'd kill myself. I wouldn't think twice about it. I'd do it that quick! [*She snatches his shoulders.*] Red, honey, I love you something awful, you've got to believe me, Red!

RED [*softly*]: Sure I do.

STAR: But you don't love me that way, do you Red? [*Pause.*]

RED: Not—now.

STAR: Do you think you'll ever?

RED [*after a pause*]: Maybe next spring sometime.

STAR [*bitterly*]: Maybe next spring sometime! It's always sometime next spring. And maybe next spring it'll be winter and maybe there won't even be any next spring! Oh, my God, Red, what do you think love is?

RED [*rising from the cot*]: Love's a warm bed to lie in when a man's through fighting. [*He goes to the window.*]

STAR: Is that all?

RED: That's all I can say it is now. There's a bunch of men in the street. The Rover boys. You'd better clear out.

STAR [*jumping up with a frightened cry*]: They're coming here! [*She rushes over to the lamp and turns it out. Torch glare comes through the window and a threatening murmur of voices.*]

RED: Take this money Luke gave me and turn it over to the men. Get out the back way.

STAR: Red!

[*He throws her across the stage to the inner door.*]

STAR: What're you going to do? [*She throws her arms around his neck.*]

RED: Nothing!

[*With a sudden crash the door is broken in and the band of terrorists enter.*]

LEADER: Come outa there, skunk!

RED [*stepping into the torch glare*]: I've been expecting you boys.

LEADER: Hope we haven't kept you waiting. [*To others.*] Tie him up.

RED: You aren't afraid of my two hands against all that artillery are you.

STAR [*wildly*]: What are you going to do with him? What are you going to do?

LEADER: One of you boys take care of the lady. [*Star is pinioned and gagged by one of the men.*]

RED: Let go of her!

[*He lurches forward. The lamp is smashed. Much noise. Star is screaming. First she is struck down near one side—then someone fires and Red falls.*]

ONE OF BAND: There's a bunch coming. We better scram out of here.

LEADER: Let 'em have it if they try and stop us! Come on!

[*They crowd out the door. Outside there is a pandemonium rising to a crescendo. Torches glare through the windows and door. There is a sudden burst of firing.*]

STAR [*pulling herself across the floor to Red's body—sobbing wildly*]: Red—Red—Red.

CURTAIN

SCENE TEN

Scene: Bram's cabin. About two months later.

Winter has broken up and it is now one of those clear, tenuous mornings in early spring. A thin clear sunlight pale as lemon-water comes through the windowpanes of the cabin which is even barer and cleaner-looking than usual in this strange light.

Fern comes slowly out of the back room. She looks very tired and worn in her plain black calico dress. She stands by the window. After a while she appears to see someone coming. She goes to the door and opens it. It is Star.

FERN: Star!

STAR: Yeah. I come to tell you good bye.

[*She steps inside, dressed gaudily as ever but her youth suddenly gone. There is a tragic dullness in her face and voice. She carries a shabby traveling case.*]

FERN: Where you going, Star?

STAR: Birmingham. I'm pulling out on that seven o'clock train. It's about time for it, ain't it?

FERN: Yes, but—

STAR: I'll set here by the window where I can see it coming. [*She pulls a chair to the window and sits down, nervously lighting a cigarette.*]

FERN: Where you going, Star?

STAR: I just told you. Birmingham.

FERN: Yes, but—

[*She seats herself uncomfortably opposite Star who avoids her eyes. Neither speaks for a moment.*]

FERN: Birmingham?

STAR: Yeah.

FERN: What're you going to do in Birmingham, Star?

STAR [*nervously*]: I dunno. Something'll turn up.

FERN: Yes, Yes, a-course it will.

STAR: I'm sick of this place. I'll be damned glad to see the last of it. [*She stands up.*] I—I guess it's nearly time for the train. I told the station man to flag it. I—I wanted to see you before I left. I haven't seen you since the night that—[*She drops her cigarette and grinds it beneath her toe.*]

FERN: What are you going to do in Birmingham, Star?

STAR [*sharply*]: I told you once already!

FERN: Oh, yes, yes, I—forgot.

STAR: There's a woman in Birmingham sent me the money. Said for me to come on up an' she'd see what she can do for me. She runs a sort of house there.

FERN: Oh. A boardin' house?

STAR: Yeah, a sort of boardin'-house. She said there might be something I could do around there til I got on my feet.

FERN: That oughta be nice.

STAR: Uh-huh. Better than nothing. I'll give you the address. Here. If you ever need something—drop me a line. I'll try to send you a little money from time to time.

FERN: Money?

STAR: I'll be making some.

FERN: I don't want money.

STAR: Red would want me to send you some. He was going to pay you back that money you gave toward the strike. Red was that kind of guy. Maybe I can pay most of it back myself if I keep working steady.

FERN: There's no call for you to give me a cent. I don't need it now.

STAR: You'll want it for Luke. He's the last of us. I—I keep thinking about something Red said—the night he got killed.

FERN: What was it?

STAR: He said the reason you give up your money was because you *seen* something all of a sudden.

FERN: Yes. That was it.

STAR: I said It seemed more to me like you'd been struck blind all at once, and he said, Yes, maybe you was struck blind for a minute. There was a lot of difference between looking at a candle and then looking at the sun.

FERN: He said that? [*She stands up, a little puzzled.*]

STAR: Yes. That's what he said. I thought I'd better tell you. Maybe you can make more sense out of it than I can, huh?

FERN: Yes. Thank you, Star.

STAR: They say the strike's about over. I guess they can thank you and Red for that! [*With passion.*] He didn't get killed for nothing! [*More quietly.*] And you didn't give your money for nothing, neither. The work'll be safer now an' I guess they'll have to pay fair wages . . . that's the train blowing. [*They both cross and meet stage center.*] I've got to be off. Good bye.

FERN: Good bye, Star. Good luck.

STAR: Thanks. I'll need it. [*She picks up her suitcase, then glances toward Bram's door. A little of her hard surface reappears.*] You can tell Bram good bye for me, too.

FERN: I will Star.

STAR [*with a harsh laugh as she runs out the door*]: You can tell him I'm gone to town to buy me a new silk kimona!

[*She goes out. In a dazed manner Fern seats herself again in the rocker. The train whistle blows more faintly, dying away. After a while Luke enters.*]

LUKE: Another truckload of rations came through just now. Look, Mother. Look at this. Half pound of fatback, two pounds of beans, cornmeal, coffee— [*He crosses to table.*] Where's Bram? He'll sure be glad to get coffee!

FERN [*dully*]: Bram went back to bed.

LUKE: He's queer in the head again this morning. He called me

John. He said he was glad to see I'd quit working up there in them Yankee mines.

[*Fern is apathetically silent.*]

LUKE: How about fixing some coffee?

FERN [*getting up slowly*]: All right. [*She walks to the inner door after having gotten the package.*]

LUKE: I'm going to the mines. I reckon the strike's about over. They say Gomstock's ready to sign. Red's getting killed stirred up such a hornet's nest around that old buzzard's head, they say he was willing to make peace at any terms! [*Then, softly.*] Mother, the men won't forget that it was your money that pulled them through.

FERN: It wasn't my money, Luke. It was yours. [*Pause. She avoids his eyes.*] Now you're going back in the mines. [*Sharply.*] That's where you're headed, ain't it?

LUKE: I guess I got to go back for a while. But maybe it won't be for good.

FERN [*grimly*]: No. Maybe not for good.

LUKE: You ain't sorry, Mother?

FERN [*harshly*]: Sorry for what?

LUKE: That you give up the money?

FERN [*bitterly*]: Naw, I ain't sorry, God help me, it was you or all the others. I'm just a bit tuckered out, that's all. There's a great—tiredness—in me. [*She moves her chair near the door.*] I'm tired clean through. [*Laughs.*] Don't pay me no mind. I'm nothin' but an old woman, without much sense . . . .

LUKE: You ain't old, Mother. [*He moves near her awkwardly trying to comfort her.*]

FERN: Ain't old? [*She laughs harshly.*] I'm as old as those everlasting hills out there! That's how old I am.

LUKE [*moving toward the door*]: I reckon the hills're old all right. But they're as strong as they ever was, ain't they? [*He opens the door.*] And they're beautiful, too. Oh, Lord, but they do look swell at sunup. It hurts you inside. It makes you stop breathin' almost . . . there's a right heavy mist this mornin. It's thick as wood smoke down in the hollow. Gosh, but you'd think that the woods was on fire with the sun shinin' through 'em like flame an' them clouds o' mist risin' away . . . now that the frog storm's over I reckon we're due to be havin' some real spring weather right soon . . . . [*He goes out. Fern pours Bram's coffee.*]

BRAM [*stumbling out of the back room and grumbling*]: Whyncha turn the lamp on? Caint see a dern thing in here. [*He moves toward Fern.*]

FERN: It's daylight, Bram.

BRAM [*groping for a chair*]: Hmmm. It must be the dead o' winter, the light's so dim. [*He gets to his chair.*]

FERN [*rising*]: No, it's almost spring again. The sun's been up an hour.

BRAM: Funny I ain't heard the whistle.

FERN: The whistle ain't blowed, Bram. The strike's still on. [*She speaks to him as though to a child.*]

BRAM: The strike, huh? Oh, yes, I keep forginnin' about the strike. Then there ain't no call to hurry I reckon.

FERN: No, take your time, Bram. Leave your coffee set for a while til it cools. I just poured it outa the pot.

BRAM: Where's the milk, Hester?

FERN: Gone. Hester's dead.

BRAM [*dully*]: Gone? Yes, I keep forginnin' about that, too. You're Fern. Where's all the others?

FERN: What others?

BRAM: John and Joel and Star.

FERN [*after a pause*]: They're all gone.

BRAM [*stirring his cup*]: All gone, huh? And Luke, where's he?

FERN [*somewhat grimly*]: He's gone, too.

BRAM: Gone with the others?

FERN: No. Luke's gone a diff'rent way from them.

BRAM: If he wanted to dig out coal anyway why didn't he stay down here where he belonged 'stead of going up to work in them damn Yankee mines!

FERN [*wearily*]: That's John you're thinking of. That's not Luke.

BRAM: Funny. I caint keep them straight in my head somehow. Where is Luke then?

FERN: He's down at the mines.

BRAM: If the boys had listened to me we'd still be workin'.

[*A whistle is heard.*]

FERN [*sharply*]: What's that, I wonder! [*She goes to door.*]

[*Bram rises with fresh vigor like an old fire-horse at the sound of an alarm.*]

BRAM: It's the whistle blowing, by God! Where's my cap and my carbon? Where did I put my powder keg last night?

FERN: Bram, you're out of your wits! Set down there and drink your coffee. You caint go out there now.

BRAM: I'm going. I . . . . [*He goes into the other room quickly.*]

FERN [*at the sound of singing in the street*]: The strike must be over. Look! They're all marching down the street. And they're singing! [*At door.*]

BRAM [*stumbling wildly about—back on stage*]: My powder keg! My pick! I'm going to the mines.

FERN: Here, Bram. Here's your keg. [*She takes it from the chest.*]

BRAM: My pick! Where's my pick!

FERN: And here's your pick! [*Also taken from the chest.*] But Bram how'll you git to the mines? You caint see, Bram!

BRAM: I'm going! [*He stumbles eagerly out into the road.*]

FERN: Wait a minute, Bram! I'd better go with you!

[*She starts to loosen her apron and brush back her hair. But as the singing grows fainter her body slackens and a tired smile settles upon her face. She drops the apron to the floor and sinks into the rocker which stands in a stream of sunlight through the open door.*]

FERN [*with the tired breathless laughter of emotional exhaustion*]: I'm too tired. I'll just set here and rest for a while. It's all over anyhow I reckon and I'm all tuckered out . . . .

[*She rocks slowly back and forth in the sunlight with a faint, tired smile on her face as . . .*]

CURTAIN

TEXTUAL NOTES

Four distinct versions of *Candles to the Sun* are known to have survived. First is the rehearsal script of *Candles to the Sun* used by actress Jane Garrett (now Jane Garrett Carter), who created the role of Star. A variant of that production script is part of the Tennessee Williams collection in the Harry Ransom Humanities Research Center (HRHRC) at the University of Texas, Austin; it is apparently the same text retyped with one or two spelling errors corrected.

Second is a shorter version, also titled *Candles to the Sun*, which looks to have been professionally typed and belongs to the papers of Donald Spoto in the Special Collections at University of California, Los Angeles (UCLA). This neatly typed post-production text was probably prepared for the submission of *Candles* to a Dramatist Guild play contest. This can be identified as a distinct version because Williams did a fair amount of cutting, thereby quickening its pace.

The third complete surviving text, titled *The Lamp*, names Joseph Phelan Hollifield and Thomas Lanier Williams as the co-authors, that bears Williams' explanatory note that every word of dialogue was his own comes from the HRHRC Williams Collection. I now suspect that the co-authored text which once lay just beneath this title page has disappeared, replaced by a very late version that was possibly used as a "working script" prior to, and perhaps during, the 1937 rehearsals and led directly to the production text. Neither Hollifield's early unfinished play, nor the play promised by the co-authors listed on the title page have survived.

The fourth text, titled *Place in the Sun*, is likely the earliest draft and thus far only an incomplete version is known. It is also housed at the HRHRC, along with a variety of scraps and fragments related to *Candles*. This may well be the earliest version of "Candles" that Williams composed once he had broken away from Hollifield and stopped consulting with him. In addition to a few fragments, only the last third of *Place in the Sun* has survived.

The text for this first published version of *Candles to the Sun* comes almost entirely from a rehearsal script passed along to me by the actress Jane Garrett, who originated the role of Star. The few errors found in Williams' spelling have been corrected silently; however all of Williams' dialectical spellings have been left intact, whether consistent or not, so that the script is a true representation of the young playwright's efforts.

p. 1 — *Scene: In a mining camp in the Red Hill Section of Alabama*

There is a Red Hills located about 30 miles north-north west of Birmingham, in the Arkadelphia/Rickwood Caverns area (and another, much larger, Red Hills is situated about 45 miles north-northeast of Montgomery beyond Watumka). One early draft page of *Candles* clearly states that the Red Hills—fictive or real—are in the Birmingham area. There are still major coalfields due west of Birmingham that give a general locus for the action

p. 17. — BRAM: " . . . them damn Yankee mines in Pennsylvainy"

This is probably another way of referring to the target of Bram's anger, which is the "damn anthracite mines in Pennsylvainy." Anthracite, a cleaner burning coal, was greatly desired by cities that wished to avoid smog and noxious unhealthy fumes; the winning competitor over any bituminous coal of such fields as the one in Red Hills—despite its higher price per ton.

p. 53 — The ending of Scene Four.

This marvelous, evocative scene ending was influenced by the playwright Williams loved most, Chekhov. Williams lifted the second-act ending of *The Cherry Orchard,* and shaped it to his own use and purpose. In *The Cherry Orchard,* it is a summer night and the moon is rising. Varya seeks her younger stepsister, Anya, and the three characters involved are out-of-doors: Anya is with Trofimov, a 30-year-old schoolteacher; and as Varya keeps calling out, "Anya, Anya," Trofimov becomes angry and says, "That Varya again. It's revolting."

p. 86 — STAR: "Don't you ever get tired of acting like a saint around here?"

In the earlier version, *Place in the Sun*, "Jesus Christ" is scratched out and "a saint" handwritten below. This change may have been an effort to blunt any readiness to label Red as a "Christ figure," or perhaps at least an allowance that an audience could come to that conclusion on its own.

PLAYWRIGHTS AND THEIR PLAYS

PUBLISHED BY NEW DIRECTIONS

WOLFGANG BORCHERT
The Man Outside

MIKHAIL BULGAKOV
Flight & Bliss

JEAN COCTEAU
The Infernal Machine & Other Plays

H.D.
Ion and *Hippolytus Temporizes*

LAWRENCE FERLINGHETTI
Routines (experimental plays)

GOETHE
Faust, Part I

ALFRED JARRY
Ubu Roi

HEINRICH VON KLEIST
Prince Friedrich of Homburg

P. LAL

Great Sanskrit Plays in Modern Translation

FEDERICO GARCÍA LORCA

Five Plays: Comedies and Tragicomedies

The Public and *Play Without a Title*

Three Tragedies:

The House of Bernard Alba

Blood Wedding

Yerma

ABBY MANN

Judgment at Nuremberg

MICHAEL MCCLURE

Gorf

CARSON MCCULLERS

The Member of the Wedding

HENRY MILLER

Just Wild About Harry

EZRA POUND

The Classic Noh Theatre of Japan

Elektra

Women of Trachis

KENNETH REXROTH

Beyond the Mountains (four plays in verse)

ANDREW SINCLAIR

Adventures in the Skin Trade
(based on the novel by Dylan Thomas)

DYLAN THOMAS

The Doctor and the Devils (film and radio scripts)
Under Milk Wood

TENNESSEE WILLIAMS

Baby Doll & Tiger Tail
**Battle of Angels*
Camino Real
Candles to the Sun
Cat on a Hot Tin Roof
Clothes for a Summer Hotel
**The Eccentricities of a Nightingale*
Fugitive Kind
The Glass Menagerie
**In the Bar of a Tokyo Hotel*
**Kingdom of Earth*
A Lovely Sunday for Creve Coeur
**The Milk Train Doesn't Stop Here Anymore*
**The Night of the Iguana*
Not About Nightingales
The Notebook of Trigorin
**Orpheus Descending*
**Period of Adjustment*
**The Red Devil Battery Sign*
**The Rose Tattoo*
**Small Craft Warnings*

TENNESSEE WILLIAMS (CONTINUED)

Something Cloudy, Something Clear

Spring Storm

Stairs to the Roof

Stopped Rocking & Other Screenplays

A Streetcar Named Desire

*Suddenly Last Summer

*Summer and Smoke

Sweet Birth of Youth

27 Wagons Full of Cotton (one-act plays)

The Two-Character Play

Vieux Carré

*available in *Volumes 1* through *8* of *The Theatre of Tennessee Williams*

WILLIAM CARLOS WILLIAMS

Many Loves and Other Plays